Sky High Taxi

by

Harriet Rogers

Books by Harriet Rogers

Small Town Taxi
(book 1 in the Small Town Taxi Series)

Sky High Taxi
(book 2 in the Small Town Taxi Series)

Taxi Scramble
(book 3 in the Small Town Taxi Series)

If you want to know what is really happening, ask the taxi driver.

This book is dedicated to Main Street America, big cities, little cities and the taxi drivers who move their people.

This book is a work of fiction. The names, characters, places and incidents are products of the writer's imagination or have been used fictitiously and are not to be construed as real. Any resemblance to persons, living or dead, or to actual events, locales or organizations is entirely coincidental.

Chapter One

"Gak!" I shrieked when a body launched headfirst through the window of my cab. It was the passenger side and he would have been my first fare of the day if he had chosen to enter feet first. Now there appeared to be a bullet hole in him and I wasn't sure about his life status. My name is Honey Walker. I drive for Cool Rides Taxi in Northampton, Massachusetts. Questionable bodies are not an everyday event.

I was planning to run him to the Amtrak station in Springfield, twenty minutes south of town. He had a paper bag, a bad haircut, paste white skin and clothes that didn't fit. A red jacket with Bill's Bar BQ and Tropical Fish embroidered across the front was loose over a stained white tee shirt. His pants were electric blue with a gold stripe. They were held up with a scarred leather belt with an off kilter cheap chrome buckle. The outfit screamed *Goodwill*. I wondered if he had chosen the red, white and blue color scheme or if it was just at the top of the free box. He leaned forward to say something. I heard a loud pop; he flopped through the open window and my brain recognized the sound as a gunshot.

A cabbie's job is to deliver the client safely, collect the fare money and, hopefully, a tip. Since I hadn't delivered and he hadn't paid, I was 0 for 2—3 if you consider the tip. I heard another gunshot and a paint chip flew off the hood of my cab. I grabbed the top half of the passenger by his frayed collar and mashed my right foot to the floor. The cab rocketed forward with the bottom half of the passenger flapping like a demented flag. The safest place I could think of was around the corner. I tightened my grip to finger numbing white, flew through a stop sign and screeched to a halt in front of the police station. It's a small town.

Two cops standing in front of the station grabbed their radios when they saw my cab with the bottom half of a limp body hanging out the window. The blood dripping down the side of the cab might have affected their reaction time. One cop pried my fingers off the fare's jacket as an ambulance rolled around the corner.

The EMT jumped out, put a finger to my fare's now even whiter throat and yelled, "I got a pulse!"

The ambulance went into full scream mode and screeched off with my fare. The other cop removed my white knuckles from the steering wheel. My heart was hammering, and I was gulping air like a beached goldfish.

In milliseconds I was inside cop central, in an interrogation room. My fare was on his way to the hospital or the morgue. I didn't know which.

The cops seized my taxi. The contents of the almost passenger's paper bag had scattered across the front seat. Lots of prescription pill bottles. He must have had some serious health issues. Now they were either more serious or didn't exist at all.

I sat for at least a million hours waiting for someone to use the interrogation room to interrogate me. There were a few donut crumbs and paper cups on the table. It was obvious what they usually used it for.

When a cop finally came through the door, it was Jon. Police Lieutenant Jon Stevens is a close personal friend. Really, really close. He didn't look happy and I was pretty sure it wasn't because his sex life was lacking.

"We need to talk." He leaned against the door frame with his arms crossed over his chest. He frowned at me. Even unhappy, all six feet of him looked outrageously good. He also looked very much in charge. Right now, that meant in charge of me. I'm not good at authority stuff. When pushed, I tend to push back. Jon looked ready to push. He also looked ready to pull his hair out in frustration.

Jon is six inches taller than me and too good-looking for his own good—or for mine. His dark blue eyes can turn from deep pools of seduction to cop flat way too fast. Lately he's been in a good mood because the city built a new police station. The old building, often referred to as a rat maze, is being turned into a parking garage. So Jon's big blue eyes have been more involved in seduction and less in cop mode. That's good for me.

At five foot six inches with curly blond hair, blue eyes and a cute turned-up nose, I'm the all-American girl next door. That is, if you live in the fifties and next door to Ozzie and Harriet.

"All you do is drive a taxi, for Christ's sake! How do all these bodies find you?"

"At least I delivered it to your door. And speaking of 'it,' did 'it' go to the hospital or the morgue?" My heart rate finally slowed to that of a hummingbird. I could talk instead of babble. I was sitting on my hands because they were shaking, and I didn't want Jon to see them.

"Hospital. Last I heard he's getting bullets removed from his body."

"So, you have some forensic evidence. All those pill bottles must tell you something. And the blood? Maybe you could wash it off my car before I take it back to the Cool Rides garage. Mona's gonna be pissed. And I didn't get paid and there might be a dent on the hood of the car. I am so toast."

Mona is our dispatcher and general guardian of the cars.

"Uh huh. You ever pick him up before? Where were you taking him?"

"No, and to the Springfield Amtrak."

"You pick up a lot of people. Any idea where he was headed on the train?"

"No, and him, I would remember. His haircut was bad, his clothes didn't fit, and he looked like he hadn't seen the sun in a long time."

"He hadn't. He just got out of county."

"County? As in jail county?"

"Uh huh."

"Then I would guess you knew I hadn't picked him up before."

"Yup."

"You are such a cop." I didn't use the word as a compliment. Jon didn't take the bait. But my hands were finally steady.

"Yup."

"So, can I have my car back?"

"Yeah. We took the bag and bottles and some blood samples. You can run it through the car wash." He grinned. "Good luck with Mona."

Jon knew the Cool Rides staff and he knew Mona would notice the ding in the hood no matter how clean I got the car. And she would be livid.

I snuck the car back to the garage, snatched the hose and scrubbed every inch clean. The missing paint chip on the hood stood out like a zit on a teenager's nose. I knew it would be fixed by the next day. Willie, the majority owner of Cool Rides, and Mona kept the cars immaculate.

I was getting ready to face the wrath of Mona when my cell rang.

"Lucille to the senior center." It was Mona. She was too busy to come out of the office.

"Okay. I'm on it." I rolled the hose back, hopped in the car and flew out of the parking lot. I was happy to put off the inevitable disapproval when Mona saw the tiny little almost non-existent bullet bing in the hood. I'm good at postponing confrontation. Jon would tell Willie anyway. Why aggravate anyone sooner?

When I got to Lucille's house, she was busy. But I smelled fresh-baked cookies, so I didn't mind.

I sat at the kitchen table and watched as Lucille tucked a curl of grey hair behind her ear. She pushed an arthritic finger around her kitchen junk drawer, rummaging through cracked rubber bands, unbent paper clips, dried-out stamps, a 9mm Glock, ammunition and silencer. She stroked the barrel of the Glock, expertly attached the silencer, shoved bullets into the handle grip and chambered a round. I bit into a chocolate chunk macadamia nut cookie, closing my eyes in bliss.

Lucille padded to the window. A rabbit hopped across the lawn. It twitched a tiny pink nose, sniffing for danger, and inched toward the garden. Lucille opened the window silently and steadied her hand on the sill. I glanced at the cookies on the plate in front of me and watched the rabbit lift its white cottontail. It left a brown pearl of excrement on the lawn. An incriminating piece of lettuce hung from its mouth. Visions of blood-drenched vegetables danced in my head. I decided not to eat lettuce if Lucille ever offered it and took another cookie off the plate. Chocolate chip walnut.

"Lucille?"

"Shh."

"Lucille! Don't…"

"Shh!" She repeated with the authority of age and experience.

I took a bite of cookie.

There was a loud pop and a chunk of grass and dirt exploded an inch from rabbit stew. The brown fluff launched itself straight up and hit the grass like a ground ball drilling through the center fielder's stomach. It didn't stop running until it was three houses down.

"Oh, good." Lucille removed the silencer. "That's Marion's yard. She loves animals. It's never good to disturb the neighbors." She smiled, popped the ammo out and returned gun, bullets, and silencer to the drawer. "So, what do you think?" She gestured at the cookie that was halfway to my mouth.

"You missed," I gurgled.

"You don't like it?"

"The rabbit."

"Well, I didn't want to kill the misguided creature." She looked indignant and swished her flower-print dress as she turned to me. "And I never miss." She sighed. "Will the cookies help me get lucky with the new geezer wheezer at the senior center? And just to be clear, torturing old ladies is that rabbit's favorite pastime."

"He's gay," I stated.

"The rabbit? And how would you know?"

"The Senior Center," I replied calmly.

"Honey, dear, you aren't keeping up, unless you're talking about the rabbit, and I wouldn't know about his orientation. We've had several new arrivals and I need to stake my claim soon or that awful Henrietta will scoop them up. Now focus. The cookies?"

My conversations with Lucille were rarely focused and usually disjointed. I was trying to think in a straight line. Lucille preferred triangles, stars, hexagons or anything that gave her brain lots of room to wander.

We first met when I drove her to the airport on her way to scatter her husband's ashes. Most of him made it through security and onto the airplane. There was a leak in the box and a little bit of him ended up in the giant ride-around airport vacuum. Some went up the nose of a drug-sniffing beagle. But that was months ago. Lucille was ready to move on with her love life. She looks like Betty White and acts like Clint Eastwood. Sometimes she seems a little vague, but I happen to know she has a steel-trap mind and is a great shot with a big gun. Rumor has it she used to work for the FBI.

Lucille pays the fare in cash, but she tips in homemade cookies. The object of her cookies and her affection is any unattached male over the age of sixty who knows that oral sex is a two-way street. She lives in a two-family Victorian side by side. Her landlord, who lives on the other side, is the same police Lieutenant Jon Stevens from my recent interview at the cop house.

Lucille rarely worries about who's in charge of her relationships since it is always her. I don't have the same luxury. Jon is an authoritative kind of guy and I'm an anti-authoritative kind of woman.

Lucille tossed her handbag onto the counter. It landed with an ominous thud. "Let's make sure I have everything we need."

Using the pronoun "we" allowed her to add to the bag's contents. She rooted around in the cavernous interior, pulling out two paperbacks. One looked like a steamy romance. The other was a copy of *War and Peace*.

"Excellent examples of fine literature. I never know what kind of mood I might be in." She held up the heavier book. "I've been trying to get through this since I was in high school."

She fished out lipstick, a nail file, and a box of condoms, followed by a purple vibrator.

"Oh, I sincerely hope I need those," she said, pointing to the condoms. "But not that." She slid the vibrator into the kitchen drawer next to the Glock. I had a brief mental image of the Glock with a condom stretched snugly over the muzzle.

She pulled out a Swiss army knife with more attachments than my email. "Not for bridge." She tossed it back to the junk drawer. "Hmm." She held up dental floss.

I shrugged. "If Julia Roberts needed it in Pretty Woman, why not?"

Lucille dropped it into a pocket and pulled out a roll of toilet paper.

"Is the supply at the senior center inadequate?" I asked.

She smiled and tossed it in the direction of the bathroom. Assorted pens, pencils and note pads were tucked inside and zipped closed. Sunglasses, reading glasses, long-distance glasses, back-up glasses, matches, a flashlight. The last went back into the drawer. Her wallet, checkbook and passport went into a side pocket.

"Now, do you think I need any more defensive weapons? I'll leave the Glock at home, but possibly the brass knuckles? The checkbook in case I lose the bridge game. The passport in case I need to leave the country. And it's a good I.D. More intimidating than a driver's license."

"Lucille, you're going to play bridge. None of the players are less than seventy years old. Where will you use the condoms? They don't even have beds in the senior center." I ignored the brass knuckles. Seniors are serious about their bridge games.

"Honey, you have no imagination. Haven't you ever done it in a dressing room?" Lucille's eyes misted. "I remember one time in New York. We were in Saks Fifth Avenue…"

"Time to go."

"Of course, these days, what with all the meds floating around, you never know when they might get it up. Too many pain killers, not enough Viagra."

Too much information, I thought as I hastily scooped everything into the oversized purse, sensing the beginning of one of our disjointed conversations. I hustled out the door.

Lucille followed reluctantly, glancing around for something more to cram into the bag.

A simple trip to the senior center probably wouldn't cause any problems between me and Jon. On the rare occasions that our professions overlapped, the results weren't pretty. A taxi is a magnet for people in a hurry. Sometimes they are more anxious to get away from somewhere than to go to somewhere. That may involve police cars in an equal hurry. We get calls from cop central telling us to please not pick up anyone in specific areas. It usually means that the anyone they are talking about is an escaped prisoner or may have just held up the local bank. Small town bank robbers are not known for their long-range plans and they occasionally forget about get-away transportation. More than one has called a cab to take them to and from a robbery. I once got the call from the cops right after I had picked up a scruffy looking character in the vicinity they were worried about. I told them to patch me through to Lt. Jon Stevens, pulled around the corner to the police station and told my fare to get out. There were three uniforms waiting.

But probably not at the senior center. My biggest ambition is to live a life free of drama, filled with music and flowers everywhere. Taxi driving has the music if I put a disc in the player. And flowers, like my life, grow wild. Unfortunately, in the two years I've been driving, the taxi has also had a high level of drama.

Still, before this morning, I hadn't seen Jon for a few days. And, to paraphrase Three Dog Night, one is a lonely number. I wouldn't mind seeing him in a more intimate setting, although Lucille might have encouraged me to seduce him on the table in the interrogation room.

We got to the senior center in five minutes. Lucille got out and heaved her bag with everything that a long-march army would ever want over her shoulder, staggered up the sidewalk and disappeared into the gathering of elders.

I headed back to the Cool Rides garage to see what Mona had on my agenda. Mona is slightly over five feet tall and guards the taxis like a pit bull. She keeps the drivers focused and on target. We always need new drivers. Some drivers, especially guys, have trouble with her dictatorial approach. I went inside to the office, hoping she might not notice the bullet bing.

"You got a train station, prepaid charge card. Kid's name is Terry," Mona growled and handed me a fare slip.

"I'm on it." I trotted back outside.

The slip gave me name, address, cell phone, time of pick-up and address of drop-off. Pickup was right away. The train station was twenty minutes down the interstate. I hustled just in case one of those pesky big rigs had turned over in the middle of the highway. Exiting the highway sent me through the nicer part of Springfield until I turned the corner to the train station. About a decade ago the station moved from a glorious

Grand Central style building to a depressing pre-fab box attached to the front of a wall made of pyramid size stones. Around the corner is one of the biggest strip clubs in the city. It's a tough part of town. Rumor is that the old station is going to be rebuilt. In the meantime, taxi drivers try not to linger.

I pulled into a space near a fire hydrant but far enough from it that if the giant stones caught fire, I wouldn't be in the way. There were no cars parked behind me. A big black caddy with tinted windows was three spaces ahead. Most of the passengers had hurriedly dispersed. Two people were left. One was a gangly sleepy-eyed teenager with too-big jeans. He was good-looking but had a veneer of grime, like he had been living on the street for a while. A big guy in a suit loomed over the kid, blocking the route to my cab. The suit's body type reminded me of a TV show I had seen about mountain gorillas—big upper body, long arms and really short legs. The teen looked stoned. But he was my fare. I needed to distract the ape in a suit and grab my passenger before he turned into a stain on the sidewalk.

"You owe me, fucking lowlife punk. Those were to sell." The suit was loud and pissed. He had an odd lisp and a nasal tone, like maybe someone had knocked out one of his front teeth and flattened his nose. I lowered both windows on the driver's side. The ape man grabbed the kid, lifting him off the ground. He shoved him against the wall and whispered something in his ear.

"Hey, someone call a cab?" I yelled.

The big guy turned and slid his right hand under his jacket. I've watched Lucille practice drawing her weapon at the shooting range. I recognized the move. But he let go of the kid when he went for his gun. In a split second the kid was on the ground and running. Luckily I had lowered the windows because the kid dove through the back one. I felt him hit the seat. The big guy was slower with his big bulk and short legs, but he was still only two steps behind. He thrust a huge arm through my open window. His other hand waved a gun. Up close and personal he smelled like a vat of mint julep. Too much aftershave. My eyes watered.

"Shit!" I yelped.

My right leg twitched, and the car lurched forward. It missed the fire hydrant by inches. Gorilla Guy didn't. I heard a couple of loud bangs and the back tire of the caddy deflated. The taxi shuddered like an NFL player shaking off a blow to the head.

The kid stuck his head back out the window. "Jesus!" He gulped and ducked back inside.

I could see the goon bent at a right angle over the hydrant. He met the top of the cast iron obstacle at crotch height. I took off up the street.

"Seatbelt?" I said to the kid when my breathing slowed.

"Yeah," he mumbled, groping for the ends. I heard a snap and turned toward the interstate.

"So, who was the suit?" I asked.

I checked him in the rearview. "Just some guy," he said leaning back against the seat. His eyes drooped closed.

I abandoned conversation. Twenty minutes later I got off the highway in Northampton. No sound from the backseat.

I turned around. The kid was tipped sideways. A string of drool hung from his mouth. He wasn't moving. I pulled over. He was white. I don't mean his racial persuasion. I mean as in no blood flow. I touched his face. Really cold. No breathing.

I smashed the accelerator down, barreled through the light and flew up the hill toward the hospital. The car screeched as it careened around the corner to the emergency room entrance. I slammed the brakes, shifted into park and stumbled inside, yelling for help.

The secretary behind the desk didn't look up. She adjusted her glasses, pulled some papers out of the drawer and slapped them onto a clipboard.

"Insurance company?" She shoved the clipboard across the counter.

"No, I mean, outside, no breath." I waved my hands wildly.

"Yes, and what is the nature of the problem?"

"Breathing, the problem is breathing."

She pointed to the clipboard. "Please fill out the section about insurance."

I sucked in my own breath. Two EMTs appeared with a rolling gurney, took a look in the backseat of my cab, loaded the unconscious kid onto the gurney and disappeared through the swinging doors.

The desk lady rushed after them squawking about insurance forms. She came back in five minutes looking depressed. She looked at me accusingly.

"Hey, I just drive," I said.

I hung in the waiting room and watched mothers wipe runny noses and stick things in screeching mouths. Someone came in with a bolt-sized nail in his shoulder and a nail gun in his hand. I heard the secretary mutter about insurance as the aides wheeled him down the hallway. Twenty minutes later I was still there when the doctor came out.

"You next of kin?" he asked.

"Delivery system." When he looked confused I added, "Taxi driver."

"Ah well, I need to call the police because drugs were involved. They might want to question you."

I groaned. If it was Jon, his questions would be about me getting in trouble driving a taxi. Again. The waiting room was depressing. I went outside figuring my time was better spent cleaning drool off the back seat of my cab.

The kid's backpack was on the floor. Two pill bottles lay on the seat. I rolled one of the pill bottles over to see the label. Oxycodone was written on it in black marker. There was one pill left, no name.

When the cruiser arrived, I didn't recognize the officer but I pointed out the bottles and backpack and explained that I headed to the hospital when my passenger was unresponsive.

"You should thank her," the doctor said as he joined us. "The kid is alive, but you won't get any information for a while. Another ten minutes and we would have wheeled him to the morgue."

The cop and the doc wandered back inside. I didn't really eavesdrop, but their voices carried.

"I don't know where this one got 'em, but there's a lot of pain killers floating around out there. Aging population, more pain, more pain killers. So, if you got any extra cash in your pocket, invest in drug companies. Overall, the pain killers do what we want. But this kid was on a joy ride. He overdosed on

something. We can run a tox on his stomach contents."
The doctor paused. "Or you can. I got 'em in a baggie
inside." The doctor smiled.

"Kid probably just raided his parent's medicine
chest. I'll talk to him. You got next of kin?"

They walked farther inside, and I couldn't hear
them. The cop talked briefly to the secretary and came
back outside.

He stuffed the kid's meager possessions into an
oversized evidence bag and took my phone number
and address.

"We may call you later. Thanks for helping." He
started back inside.

"Are you going to investigate the drugs this kid
got hold of? I mean, just in case?"

"In case what?" The uniform looked at me like I
was a flea on his backside. Annoying but not usually
lethal. Of course, I could be like the fleas that carry
bubonic plague.

"It's an overdose. Kid raided someone's medicine
stash. I'll talk to him about it."

"What if he stole it or someone sold it to him?"

"You been listening in where you weren't
supposed to. Keep driving that taxi and leave the law
to the professionals."

I felt like I had been patted on the head like a good
puppy. I wanted to give the professional a good head
slap. I could make sure the kid was okay later.

I never took anything stronger than aspirin and
wondered what kind of high came from oxycodone. I
shrugged and called in to see if I had another fare.

"You got Herman Wolenski. Have a great time.
How'd the train ride go?" Mona said.

"You should check that pay ahead card. It might have been stolen."

"What? What the hell happened and where are you?"

"I'm fine, car is fine. Passenger is lucky. I'll tell you when I finish with Herman."

"As long as there's no damage." She meant to the car.

I took off to get Herman, grateful that I had another fare to keep me busy.

Herman is elderly and needs a lot of medical trips. Sometimes he has real problems and sometimes he's just desperate for company. He gets in the cab with a bag full of meds. Herman returns drugs the way I return shoes. He has whole lists of ailments, treatments, side effects and results. He talks non-stop about his medical problems. When I'm done with Herman, I imagine I have a dozen life-threatening ailments. And he doesn't tip.

He was outside the cottage in the retirement village leaning on his walker. His thin gray hair was slicked back and suspenders held baggy pants somewhere just below his chin.

"What took you so long? And don't even think about helping me. Just 'cause you're young doesn't mean you know everything. I can open the door. Don't need no help from someone barely outta diapers." He hurled the walker at me and backed his skinny butt into the front passenger seat. "Don't tell me about seatbelts. I don't like 'em and I don't use 'em. I lived a lotta years without 'em, never put my head through the windshield."

"Herman, I can't take you anywhere without your seatbelt on." I reached over to buckle him in and he slapped my hand. We went through this every time I gave him a ride.

"I can do it myself. Stop feeling up my privates. I know what you're after."

I got in the driver's side, buckled up and we sat until Herman gave in and fastened his seatbelt.

"They gave me some sorta stuff for my back. Wasn't even my back that hurt, it was my knees. And my elbow. Knocked it when the stupid dog next door bumped into my walker. Someone oughta do something about that damn critter. They gave me that Oxy stuff. Supposed to kill the pain. Didn't do anything I could tell, so I gave it away. Well, maybe I gave a little bit to the dog. Haven't seen him since." He chuckled. "And that kid next door, swapped him some for a bottle of Jack Daniels. Now that killed the pain. Well, maybe I kept some pills for me. Only medicine I need is that stuff for my diabetes. And the rat poison to thin out my blood. And some weird pill that's supposed to help my bowel movements."

Too much information, but I keep my mouth shut when I'm transporting Herman. He likes to talk, not to listen. It took us ten minutes of non-stop, one-way conversation to get to the doctor's office. I dropped Herman and headed back to Cool Rides. The only words I uttered were to tell the receptionist to call when Herman was ready to be picked up.

When I pulled into the parking lot, three other cabs were lined up. Belle, my best friend and an excellent cabbie, was back from her first run. I had discovered a few interesting things about Belle in the year I had known her. She had a college degree, she had invested money from her previous employment well and that employment was the oldest profession in the world, possibly the universe.

We always have more cars than drivers, so Mona ran an ad for new help. We got the usual scary applicants, but a guy named Rigger made the grade. He had experience driving cab and was big with lots of muscle. That pleased Willie, the co-owner of Cool Rides, because the big guy could go into weird places after dark. I always told Willie I could go anywhere, anytime, but he was not happy sending women into combat. In the wee hours, the train station in Springfield could be deadly.

Belle was outside with the new guy, vacuuming cars. Belle retired from her career as a prostitute when her pimp/husband was murdered. She's six feet of mocha brown woman with an additional few inches of Afro. She has a face like an angel and a mouth like a pissed off gang banger. My attitude is wimpy by comparison.

"Rigger, huh?" She cast an appreciative glance at his muscle. He was wearing a tight black tee shirt with THE WAR ON STUPID IS LOSING written across the front.

"Yeah." Man of few words. He smiled at me.

"As in, you rigged the game or rigor mortis?" asked Belle.

"Belle!" I really didn't want to lose another driver.

Rigger grinned. "Nope. As in big rig, eighteen-wheeler, large truck."

"Mom think she was hit by a truck when she pushed you out her bottom drawer?" Belle flipped off the vacuum.

"I was conceived at a truck stop."

"That would have been my second guess."

"At least she didn't name me eighteen-wheeler." He grinned at Belle.

She grinned back.

Rigger pulled a plastic baggie from under one of the seats. "So, what do we do when we find something?"

"Lost and found is inside," I said, examining the bag. I sniffed the contents. "Dumpster," I said. "It's not oregano."

Rigger shrugged. "The raccoon population will thank us."

The local wildlife population had moved into downtown, closer to the dumpsters. As a food source, we were on the "A" list. Add suburban sprawl and the wildlife had deserted the 'burbs. Black bears, raccoons, skunks, possums were regulars. The parking commissioner had looked up one day into the eyes of a moose.

When he first came to town, Rigger had stumbled across a pair of skunks in an alley. They were more interested in the dumpster than in him, but he now knew the habits of the local animal wildlife population. The human wildlife was also part of every cabbie's work day.

"So, what's on for this afternoon?" I asked Belle.

"Ha, you get to take Herman home. I'm getting Ann Washington to the doctor."

20

I groaned. Another ten minutes of listening to what might be wrong with Herman and hoping it wasn't wrong with me, too.

When I arrived, Herman was outside looking furious.

"Said I'm not drinking enough water. Dehydration! We got to go to the store and get me some bottled water."

"Okey, dokey." Off to the local grocery.

When we got to his cottage, I lugged bags of pills, water, milk, orange juice and soda inside.

Herman's apartment reflected Herman. Boring, cheap and old. A veneer coffee table was next to a plaid recliner that was painfully close to a television. The recliner fabric had burn holes from when Herman used to smoke. Rows of pills lined the coffee table, divided into groups with each group on a piece of paper with the day of the week printed on it. Still, sometimes Herman forgot to look at the pieces of paper. Growing old is not for the weak, I thought.

Herman unpacked the new pills. There was a lot of Oxycodone.

I picked up a bottle. "Where does this one go?"

"Just stick it anywhere. I gotta take it every day. You ever try that stuff? Oxy whatever?"

"Ah, no."

"Well, you should. One pill makes some of the pain go away, just not enough. Two pills and you could squash your toe with a hammer and smile about it. Three pills you'd be on your way to heaven. Or wherever you're gonna go."

I thought about the kid at the emergency room and wondered how close he came to heaven and if anyone

21

would make sure he didn't get there if he got his hands on more drugs. And where did he get those drugs? And who was the big guy at the train station and what did he say to the kid? And did the cop who was going to "talk to him" help? Did Jon know what happened? Giving myself a mental lecture on being stupid, I knew I should stay out of it.

Herman mumbled. "Gotta take that for high blood pressure, that kills the pain, that keeps the shit moving, that keeps my iron up. Might as well eat a fry pan. Hit myself over the head with it to kill the pain in my back. I need you to pick me up day after tomorrow in the afternoon. I'm taking all this crap and they need my blood. Bunch of vampires. Hardly any blood left in me. Don't need to thin it out anymore."

"What time?"

"One o'clock. And be on time, fer Christ's sake. I can't eat 'til they drain me. Can't even have coffee so don't bring any with you. I don't want to even smell the dang stuff."

I left him arranging pill bottles. I wondered if Lucille took any medication.

I spent the rest of the afternoon running errands for people who didn't have cars and didn't want them. Toilet paper, liquor, coffee and aspirin were in high demand. When I got home, there was a message from Jon on my answering machine.

"Call me."

Did I want to see Jon? You betcha. Was I going to respond to an order like that? I'd think about it. Giving orders was natural for Jon. Taking them wasn't natural for me. I might just take my day off to go see the kid in the hospital.

22

Chapter Two

The next day was my day off. After haphazardly cleaning the apartment, I checked out the new shoe arrivals at the downtown stores. There was a pair of spikes with little bells on them. I pulled out the charge card. I could ask Belle what she thought before I tested them out in front of Jon. By noon, I had talked myself into walking to the hospital and checking up on Terry, the kid who had tried to reach Heaven sooner rather than later.

In a new, enlightened visiting policy the hospital has decided that any visitor is usually a good visitor and social interaction will help the sick heal faster. The visiting hours are pretty much anytime unless the patient is restricted. Except in ICU which was where the shooting victim I had delivered to the police remained.

"Room 217," the receptionist said.

As I stepped off the elevator and started down the hall, the door to room 217 opened. I recognized the big guy from the train station. He turned and noticed me staring at him. With an angry frown, he strode to the stairs and slammed through the door. I hurried down the hall to Terry's room.

"Hi," I said as I pushed the door open. The kid was propped up in the hospital bed staring out the window. There was no one else in the room. I hadn't looked at his face very closely when I was driving, and

23

I didn't look at all when he was wheeled away into the bowels of the E.R. He was maybe fourteen or fifteen years old but might pass for older or younger from a distance.

Blond hair fell into his eyes and he pushed it back nervously. "Who're you?"

"I picked you up at the train station. You drooled in my cab."

"Oh, yeah. Sorry." He gave me the teenage stare. Blank mixed with hostility.

"So, what happened?" I asked.

"Ask the doctor. He won't tell me anything. Keeps asking who he should call. I keep telling him, nobody."

"You were coming up here to visit someone, right? They must be worried that you haven't arrived."

"Yeah, that was mostly a way to get out of the city."

"Someone paid your tab with a credit card."

"Uh huh," he said with enough attitude to make me wonder if the card was bouncing like a beach ball.

"Am I going to get burned for that fare?"

"Hey, doesn't Visa pay no matter what? Like if you get authorized or something? Besides, that's between you and the card guys."

"You're being kind of a shit considering that I saved your ass from riding those pain killers to hell." A little teenage angst goes a long way and I was getting tired of the attitude.

"Oh, yeah, like I wanted to be brought down. The guy on the train told me I could ride that stuff all the way to Heaven and back. What the hell? I figured I'd give it a try. If one got me high, two would get me

24

higher. And, you know what? It did. And the next thing I know I'm waking up with my throat on fire and tubes in every hole in my fuckin' body. So, what was the favor you did for me?"

"So, you got the stuff from some guy on the train? Where'd you come from?"

"Like I said, the city. What's it to you anyway?"

I moved in closer. "Like I said, I don't want to get burned for that fare." I wondered if the hospital was going to get burned. The kid obviously wasn't insured. But this was Massachusetts where everyone is insured. The hospital would collect from the state eventually, maybe. I had spent some time on the street when I was a lot younger. I had a little sympathy for his situation.

"Whatever," he said and stared out the window.

"Yeah, whatever," I said. I couldn't decide how much I cared. Mostly I was curious. Who would give that kind of drug to a fifteen-year old kid? "So, who was the guy that grabbed my cab, and was it the same guy who just left your room?"

"What guy? You should leave me alone. I didn't ask you to bring me here. You were supposed to take me to someone's house."

"You were unconscious! What, you wanted me to shove you out the door? And that address was an empty lot. I checked. Who were you going to meet?"

"They woulda come got me. I woulda been fine. But you had to be Miss Stick-your-nose-in and bring me to a fuckin' hospital."

The kid was right, time to leave. "Don't be an asshole for the rest of your life," I said and closed the door.

25

When I got to the Cool Rides office the next morning, everyone was sitting around the new humongous flat screen TV. Rigger was wearing a black tee shirt with MY PHONE IS SMARTER THAN YOUR PHONE emblazoned across the front. A boxed set of the British automotive comedy Top Gear—the full season—lay on the coffee table. On TV, the stars were chasing each other around the race track in oversized buses and other vehicles to prove that mass transit could get you there on time. The double-decker bendy bus finally tipped over, lying on its side like a dried-out worm.

The Cool Rides phone rang. My day had begun. When I had passed the taxi on the way into the office, I noticed the paint chip bullet bing had been repaired. Mona hadn't said anything. Willie must have told her not to. Maybe Jon had explained how it wasn't my fault.

Mona answered the phone, conferred briefly with Willie and handed him a fare slip. She came back out to what we referred to as the driver's lounge. "That's an airport. Willie will take it. Everyone else go uptown and see what you can scare up."

It was a tactic that Mona used to break in new drivers.

Go uptown and see who hangs where and which section of Main Street might provide the most paying fares. Belle and I knew the territory. Northampton had once housed a state mental hospital. The property was now luxury and mixed-use condos but the precedent had been set and the city was host to a large community of mental health services and, thus, service recipients. Combine those recipients with students

26

from a high-end college and the streets were a good show and a great place to panhandle for quarters and coffee. A taxi driver's job was to sort out the paying fares from the "HOW MUCH?" people and get the maximum number of customers to their destinations in the minimum amount of time while occasionally collecting some tips. Knowing the regulars, not to mention who was where in their meds cycle, was important when one was working the city center area. The entire downtown is only six blocks long. Getting the lay of the land is easy but important.

I drove to upper upper Main Street and trolled for anyone who had missed one of the not-always-predictable buses. That might be students trying to get to the university or a working stiff heading south to the larger cities. The bus stop is next to Dunkin Donuts. I indulged in a super mocha with whip, butterscotch, chocolate topping, and an extra shot of espresso while I waited to see which bus was late.

Belle headed to middle upper Main. Starbucks groupies and people at the beginning of their meds cycle hang there. As cabbies, we avoid the heavily medicated people. They don't always know where they're going and sometimes don't have the money to go there anyway. And they never tip.

Farther down Main Street crowds increase in size.

Middle Main is mostly shoppers and people at the top of their meds cycle. When the meds kick in they can handle bigger crowds. They're more functional and understand that they have to pay for a ride. They still don't tip. Lower middle Main is reserved for the homeless who are generally quiet and not looking for taxi rides. If they need one, the homeless shelter will call ahead, and we pick them up there. The shelter pays and tips. Lower Main is the staggeringly drunk. We don't pick them up ever; they create a variety of problems from a cabbie's viewpoint. Pedestrians wander everywhere, unaware of the concept of crosswalks. It's a driver's nightmare, but it's in Technicolor and it's fabulously entertaining.

Two hours later, Belle and I were back at Cool Rides. I had taken one student to the mega mall in Holyoke. Belle had ferried three separate rides to the Vet's administration.

Ten minutes later, Rigger pulled in.

"So, you get any rides?"

"Three rides, one fare," he stated morosely. "I got burned by a little old lady who needed to get home from the dentist. She went in to get the fare money and I never saw her again. There was a back door. Who'd have thought she could move so fast?"

"Did you figure out Main Street?" Belle smiled.

"Oh yeah. Lots of crazies. Pulaski Park to the railroad underpass. Working poor, students, drug deals, beginning of meds cycle, top of meds, end of meds and alcoholics, with crazies mixed in everywhere. Jay-walking is the city's official sport. Did I get it right?"

"Yup. Just don't say it out loud. It ain't politically correct." Belle grinned.

Rigger looked up from cleaning out the back of the cab. "I met JoJo."

"Yeah?" Belle smirked. "He have his flute?"

"Uh huh. And his whole band. Whenever he stopped playing the flute he got into a fight with the band."

28

"Nothing wrong with that. They don't play very well anyway," Belle said with a grin.

"They don't play at all. And since no one else can see them and he was in the middle of the street, he was putting a major crimp in the traffic flow. I think the cops took him to the hospital to adjust his meds."

"So, by next week he should be able to hang with the middle Main crowd."

"I guess," Rigger said and fished a pair of pink panties out of the back seat. "Dumpster?"

"Unless you want to wear 'em," said Belle.

I had Herman in ten. I quickly checked the cab for items left behind. I really didn't want Herman finding someone's thong or any underwear. There was a black mesh bag containing red lipstick, a super-sized box of condoms, a purple thong with red feathers hanging from the butt and a starched nurse's cap. I tossed it all into the lost and found and wondered if the student I picked up was working her way through college. Then I got a gas card from Mona and headed off to gas up and get Herman.

Herman's cottage was off a side street. At first, the flashing lights didn't worry me; the presence of an ambulance at the retirement village was a daily affair. Then I got closer and realized they weren't the red of the ambulance but the multi-color of a police cruiser. The ambulance was there but its lights were off. Never a good sign. I rounded the corner and almost ran over Lieutenant Jon Stevens.

I down buttoned the window as he walked over to the driver's side.

"What are you doing here?" I smiled.

29

"What are you doing here?" Typical cop. Answer a question with a question.

"Pick up."

"Police business."

Now that neither of us had provided any vital information, maybe we could talk about something important. Like how I could collect my fare with all those police cars in the way.

"What police business?"

"Unattended death." That meant someone had died outside the hospital with no doctor hanging around to sign the exit papers and make sure the insurance was up to date. The police then came and made sure it was all natural and organic.

"Who died?" I asked, realizing we were in front of Herman's unit. The door opened, and a gurney came out with the ever-ominous body bag on it. "I was picking up Herman. I don't have a fare, do I?"

"When did you last speak to Herman?" Jon was in cop mode.

"Day before yesterday when I dropped him off."

"Did you go inside?"

"Yeah, groceries," I said, and Jon nodded. He understood the cabby's duties pretty well. He had driven with most of us for a variety of reasons. We covered a lot of miles and saw a lot of human interaction. Sometimes the cops were interested.

"I need you to come inside and see if you notice anything different. You were probably the last one to see Mr. Wolenski alive."

I got out of the car and followed Jon, now in full police mode, inside. I looked around the small apartment. It didn't smell too good, mostly like I imagined death smelled—a combination of stale odors and fresh excrement. It seemed relatively peaceful. There was no sign of a struggle, no blood, nothing broken. In fact there wasn't much there at all. The TV, the recliner, the clean coffee table sat right where they were the day before.

"You collected his meds?" I asked, assuming the tech guys sent them to the lab.

Jon stared at me.

"What?" I stared back.

"What meds?" asked Jon. "The scene is just the way we found it. I haven't checked the bathroom yet."

"No, he kept his meds right next to his recliner. They were arranged on pieces of paper with the day he needed to take them written on each paper so he wouldn't get mixed up. There were a lot of meds."

"Did you notice names on the bottles? Any pain killers? I'm going to need to get hold of his doctor." Jon was thinking out loud.

"I dropped him off at Northampton Medical Center. I don't know which doctor he used." I looked around the apartment. It was pretty basic. No photographs of family, no artwork, no mementoes of any kind. In our business we go through a lot of clients who drop dead, not completely unexpectedly. Senior citizens give up their cars and need transportation. We go to a lot of funerals. Sometimes the whole staff goes. Sometimes not. I knew I would be attending Herman's, probably alone.

"You have his next of kin to notify?" I looked at Jon.

"I just got here ten minutes before you did. You know who his next of kin is? The retirement home would have the list, I guess."

"Yeah, they're the ones who reported it. One of the personal care people came to help him get ready for you. So, thanks for looking at the scene." I was being told to leave.

"Yeah, okay." I headed for the door.

"Hey, Honey."

"What?" I snapped. Jon's orders were beginning to push my buttons.

"You stopping by tonight?"

"Are you inviting me?" I paused. "And what's for dinner?"

"Pizza, beer and a big screen TV."

"Do I get the remote?"

Jon smiled. "Maybe."

"Maybe," I replied.

As I walked to my taxi, I noticed a piece of paper in the bushes. It was one of Herman's days of the week. I pointed it out to the uniform standing by the door.

"Make sure 'Mr. I'm-in-charge' gets this. It might have some bearing on what he's doing."

I went back to Cool Rides and explained the situation to Mona.

"You get funeral duty. I only knew him on the phone and that wasn't any treat."

I sighed. Cool Rides sort of prided itself on a good record of funeral attendance as our customers moved on. So I was up.

"Right now, you got a pickup. Lucille wants to go back to the senior center."

This was good; Lucille always cheers me up. When I got there, she was in the midst of a purse-packing episode, packing the maximum amount of stuff that she may or may not need into her oversized shoulder bag. She recently thought about downsizing because she thought her posture was becoming lopsided. But she couldn't fit enough into a smaller bag.

"Hey, Lucille, how's the bunny population?"

"Too big, but they're fast learners. They haven't been through the lettuce recently." She rummaged around and extracted her copy of *War and Peace.*

"This is too heavy." She pulled an oversized butcher's knife from her cutlery drawer. Opening the book to page 203, she raised the knife. Her hand went up and down in a blur. With a thunk she split the spine and the book was two-thirds shorter.

"I will finish this book. Just not all at once. I'll come back for the rest later." She crammed the first 203 pages into the bag.

"Maybe it's time for an electronic reader," I offered cautiously.

"God forbid."

We got into the cab and headed for the senior center.

"Lucille?"

"Yes, dear?"

Given the number of funerals I've been to I should know how to handle the death thing better.

"Did you know Herman Wolenski?"

"Humm?"

"Herman Wolenski. Did you know him?"

"Oh, Herman, he's a thoroughly unlikeable person. Always complains, takes too much medication, just can't be nice."

"Not anymore."

"What?"

"I said, not anymore. Herman died last night."

"Oh, well. We're all getting older. He probably said something nasty to the Grim Reaper."

"I have to go to his funeral."

"Oh, how unfortunate. I hope Willie won't force any of you to come to my funeral."

It was Willie's policy, and, in fairness to me, a sense of responsibility or guilt, that was forcing me to see Herman put in the ground. I remembered that Herman had mentioned a brother who lived on the West Coast. Willie or Mona would find out and let me know the details.

"I was kind of thinking you might want to go with me. I don't have a date."

"What about the other drivers? Or Jon?"

"Jon is in cop mode and none of the other drivers knew Herman. Mona said it was up to me."

"I'll check my wardrobe. I'm quite certain I had my widow's black dry-cleaned. When is the event?"

"After the autopsy. The police probably want a tox screen to see how much of his meds he had been taking. His brother will decide when and where."

"Well, fine. Now, perhaps I should do a bit of shopping on the way to the senior center. I'd like to stop at Guns and Daisies. I need some ammunition for my Glock and flowers for the kitchen table. I can order something for Herman's service as well. Then we need a quick stop at Oh! My to pick up batteries for my vibrator." She stared into space for a few seconds. "And I might pick up one of those mini vibrators for travel. Emergencies, you know."

I'm never sure when Lucille is serious. She's a regular at Guns and Daisies. And I dropped her at Oh! My, our upscale porn store, frequently. Shopping is good when faced with a tragic, or even not so tragic, death. We headed off to look over the latest in semi-automatic ammo.

When we pulled in, the only other vehicle in the lot was a four-wheel drive mega truck in cherry red. It had a roll cage, chrome wheels and enough antennae to show that there was a lot more than a CD player inside. There were probably other bells and whistles, but it was too far off the ground to see.

The bell tinkled when we entered. The right side of the store was made up of glass-topped display cases filled with guns. Larger weapons hung on the walls. Shelves of ammunition lined the remaining right-hand wall space. The left side of the shop had a cooling unit full of roses. Tin buckets packed with other kinds of flowers covered the rest of the floor. A cash register and charge card machine sat on the line between the two sides with two clerks on opposite sides of the line. There was a big guy leaning against the flower counter talking to the sales clerk. He sported low-slung jeans, a wife-beater tee shirt that declared I AM A Bubba across the front, and ratty sandals. His head was shaved, and tattoos covered his arms and parts of his head. He fit the saying on his tee shirt, but I couldn't figure out why he would want to advertise it. Lucille went to the gun display first. I hung back by the door contemplating the Bubba's statement and wondering why his pants didn't fall down around his knees. I can't figure out how those guys walk, or even move, without mooning the whole world. I wanted to give the pants a jerk just to see what would happen. I tucked my hands in my jean pockets.

The clerk from the gun side looked up.

"Why, Miss Lucille, how are you? It's been too long. How is the rabbit population?" The salesman was middle-aged with receding hair. He was neatly dressed and knew Lucille well.

"Not growing as fast as it would like to, I'm sure. I keep them quite busy."

"So, you need more ammunition?"

"Yes, but I'm also looking for a new gun, something smaller, maybe more feminine. I have a date to go target shooting. My date can use my Glock, but I want something more feminine."

"Ah." The man behind the counter winked at her. "We have a whole new line called pink packers." He moved to a case full of smaller guns and accessories. There was a quick draw bra holster which I couldn't figure out, pink shooting glasses, fuzzy pink ear covers and a pink and black leather shoulder holster. He lifted out the ear covers, one of the guns, and some ammunition. "Hold this and see what you think. It's called a pink lady snubbie."

"Oh, it's quite cute."

"We can go out back and try a few rounds if you like."

Lucille put on the ear covers and passed the gun back and forth from hand to hand.

The low-slung blue jeans Bubba was sniffing roses.

36

I leaned against the door jam and yawned. I'm not a big gun fan. Mostly I'm afraid I might shoot myself by accident.

"How much this gonna run me for a dozen?" asked the Bubba.

"Those are tea roses and a dozen would cost twenty-five dollars." The flower clerk gently touched the delicate blooms.

"Huh? That much? So, what can I get for, let's see..." He emptied his pocket of several crumpled singles and tossed them on the counter. "That much."

"Well, you could get one stem for two dollars with a little bit of baby's breath to pretty it up, and an elegant white ribbon holding it all together."

Lucille laid the gun on the counter and wandered over to the larger display. The gun clerk drifted with her.

"My girlfriend wants a dozen roses," Bubba growled.

"We have some less expensive flowers, like daisies. Those are only ten dollars for a very nice bouquet." The flower clerk was small, thin and not at all muscular. He fidgeted nervously in front of the growling bubba.

"I need those roses. See, I might've sort of offended her somehow. She has a thing about the word fuck. Said I used it too much, like I have a one-word vocab she said." Bubba leaned forward onto the counter.

Across the room, Lucille held another, larger gun. The girly gun lay where she had left it.

Low-slung jeans loomed over the flower clerk. Then he spied the girly gun lying alone on the counter. He snatched it and pointed it at the clerk.

"And I'm takin' 'em. You can keep the three bucks. Or maybe you should gimme some money. Yeah, gimme whatever you got," he growled, waving the gun around.

Lucille and the gun clerk came back toward the flower side and were watching Bubba. The gun clerk looked alarmed. Lucille calmly moved over to her purse.

Bubba focused on the flower clerk.

Lucille turned back with her own Glock in her hand.

"That gun isn't loaded. Any idiot knows that you don't load up inside," she said, lowering the Glock.

"Yeah, you old bag, but I got this." And he pulled a very large knife out of his belt. "And I bet you don't know how to use that," he snarled, pointing at the Glock.

I wondered what he thought this particular old bag was doing in a gun store. Then I thought maybe stupid was multiplying faster than smart.

"Old bag? They say growing old isn't for sissies. Young man, life is not for sissies." Lucille raised the Glock.

Note to self, *respect your elders*. By the time they get to Lucille's age they are definitely not sissies.

Chapter Three

I tried to protest what I knew Lucille was going to do.

I was too late.

She chambered a round and shot Bubba's pinky toe. The explosion blasted through the silence of the store, bouncing off the walls and echoing in my brain. I grabbed my ears. The gun clerk staggered back against the wall, hands over his heart. The flower salesman fell down behind the counter. The guy with one less toe screamed and fell to his knees and then flipped onto his back.

Lucille turned and stalked back to the other side of the store.

"I'll take the snubbie." She glanced back at the bubba who rolled around on the floor clutching his foot. "And, young man, remember, never bring a knife to a gun fight." She took off the fuzzy pink ear covers and pulled out her MasterCard.

The would-be robber scrabbled to his feet and limped out the door without losing his pants. The bullet was embedded in the wooden floor.

"Should I call the police? Or an ambulance?" I asked. "With that monster truck he won't be hard to find."

"That's my truck," said the flower clerk.

By the time we left, everyone was smiling except, of course, the hold-up guy. And he didn't count because we had no idea where he was. No one had called the police and Lucille said if he could run out the door he didn't need an ambulance. She ordered a bouquet of chrysanthemums for Herman's funeral and took the tea roses for herself.

"They'll bring me fond memories," she said to the flower clerk.

"I think I'll take my truck out for a drive," he replied.

I dropped Lucille at the senior center to firm up plans for her shooting date. Guns and Daisies had been exciting. She skipped the porn store, mentioning she had plenty of supplies from there anyway. She had a spring in her step as she entered the house of elders.

I went back to Cool Rides to see if any fares had come up.

There were piles of them. Everyone wanted to go to the doctor, the grocery store, the liquor store, the porn store, Jimmy's towing, or the parking clerk, all at the same time. One guy wanted me to take him to a drug buy in a dark alley and wait to for him to finish the transaction. When I picked him up, I saw the bulge in his jacket and told him to call someone else for the return trip. He was what we call a *shove and run*. You collect the fare money when he gets in the car, shove him out at the destination and drive like hell back to home base. Then you put his number on the Do Not Pick up List.

Belle had snagged an airport pick up and Rigger had gone along to learn the ropes. I was left with a lot of pissed-off people whose cars wouldn't start or had been towed or who lost their driving privileges or maybe didn't want their own cars shot by a pissed-off drug dealer. None of them tipped, except the drug dealer who tried to pay and tip in painkillers. I declined. An outraged "How much???" was the most conversation I had with any of the others. I returned to home base with my fare money and no tips.

Belle and Rigger were back from the airport, sitting in ratty plastic lawn chairs in front of the garage, watching joggers on the bike trail that runs near the Cool Rides office. A well-endowed woman went by and Rigger's head bobbed in time with the jiggling of her breasts.

Belle elbowed him and said, "When she hits fifty, her knockers will be at her knees and she'll be poppin' pain pills like popcorn."

Rigger nodded. "Gotta do something to keep in shape."

I decided to relax before finishing the clean out and detailing of my car. Each car gets checked at the end of the day for junk and human remains.

I looked at Belle. Big, but not overweight. Rigger is built like his namesake but again, it's all muscle.

"So, what do you guys do to keep in shape?" I asked.

Belle grinned. She raised her arm and flexed a bicep. She turned her back to me and wiggled her butt. She turned back and lifted her boobs.

"See these? There's a pile of muscle behind all that lovely. And I intend to keep it there. Rigger and I have just become exercise buddies. We lift weights together."

Rigger looked over at her. "In the gym! And use the stationary bike and shit like that. I wouldn't want my knockers at my knees."

41

I lifted an arm and sighed. It wasn't saggy but no cute bump of muscle appeared when I tried to flex. I didn't even look down at my breasts.

Belle put a finger on my unmuscle. "Well, your knees won't knock, but your knockers will never be at your knees either. Too small. Honey you could dress them up as fried eggs for Halloween."

Rigger smiled at me. "Hey, the guy who counts likes 'em. Your cute lieutenant licks his lips every time he sees 'em. He has to put his hands in his pockets to avoid embarrassing himself."

I really liked Rigger.

I heaved myself out of the uncomfortable plastic chair and dragged the vacuum out to my car. The back seat yielded some pretty purple capsules. I sucked them up into the vacuum and deposited the whole mess in the dumpster. More stoned raccoons for a day or two.

It was almost quitting time when my sometimes-favorite police lieutenant pulled into the parking lot. He sauntered over.

"We need to talk." This was addressed to me but he was also looking over Rigger.

"Hi, I'm Rigger Rogers." Rigger extended his hand.

Jon shook it. "Ah, Mona found someone who meets her high standards."

"Mostly I just stood out from the crowd," said Rigger as he wandered toward the office.

Belle grinned. "Yeah, we had three felons, two registered sex offenders, one person who walked into the desk and still claimed 20-20 vision, and some weird guy who wouldn't get up off his hands and knees. Oh yeah, and the lady with the tattoos."

Having missed the job interviews, I wondered what the problem with her tattoos could be. Mona had a few tatts herself.

"Nothing wrong with nice tatts," I murmured.

"That was all she had," said Belle. "Not a stitch of clothing. Not even shoes. Now, how was she gonna drive without shoes? And who would trust a woman without shoes?" Belle was famous for her shoe collection. She had spike heels that made my soul weep with envy and my feet just weep.

Jon shifted his body closer to mine. "I want to interview you at headquarters about the piece of paper you found near Herman's cottage. And I would like a sketch of the inside of his house when you were last there."

"So, what did you find out? What killed him?"

"I need more information."

Jon was deep in cop mode. I hated that. He would ask a million questions and not answer any. We were checking schedules to see if I could show up officially when Rigger walked out the office door with a fare slip and Mona yelled to Belle.

"Judge Witherspoon wants a ride. You're up, Belle."

"Give it to Honey. I got stuff to do. The cars need washing." Washing cars was a priority for Mona and she would usually let anyone willing to wash off the hook from driving.

"Sorry, he requested you." Belle also knew that when any driver was requested, they took the fare unless Mona thought it was something weird. In this

43

case, Judge Carlton Witherspoon was trying to get a date with Belle. Belle was resisting because she felt his discovery of her previous profession would end the relationship badly, so why bother starting it in the first place? She was convinced the Judge could go up the professional ladder, but a former prostitute probably wouldn't be invited along for the ride. Mona was siding with the Judge who was, in her opinion, a good catch even if it didn't last.

Belle sighed.

"I think you should go out with him," I whispered.

"I think everyone should mind their own damn business." Belle glowered.

"If he turns out to be an idiot, just tell him you're dating Rigger."

"One, I already know he's not an idiot and second, your gaydar is off. Rigger moved to Massachusetts to get married—to Henry."

"Seriously?" I stared over at Rigger, the super muscle man who would turn most straight women's heads. Massachusetts was one of a handful of states in which same sex marriage was not only legal but encouraged by local merchants. The more weddings, the more flowers, tuxes, bridesmaids' dresses, bridal gowns, catered events...well, the list goes on. Any good capitalist knows it by heart. There's a whole industry built on it.

"Wow, I really missed that one. Have you met Henry yet?"

"Yeah, he's even nicer than Rigger. He works up at the hospital."

"As?"

"ER doc. Busy saving lives."

I wondered if I had met him when I emergency-dropped Terry.

Belle stood up and headed inside to get car keys.

"Be nice," I called after her.

She gave me a one-fingered salute.

Jon turned back to me. "Tomorrow before your first run? You could stay at my house tonight and I'll give you a ride to work in the morning."

"When are you getting cause of death?"

"Not relevant."

"Hey, if I'm giving you something, you need to give back."

"Yeah, and I will if you spend the night at my place."

"Right." I frowned. "I have some thoughts on the case that might help."

Jon looked at me. "You've been thinking about the Herman Wolenski case?"

"Well, yeah. I mean, he was my client. He wasn't nice but he was talkative. And I listen well."

"I'll tell you cause of death if you tell me everything he said, did or thought about doing."

"Deal. So, when do you get cause of death? Not to repeat myself."

"Tomorrow."

"And you will tell me?"

"What did Herman say to you?" Jon still hadn't said yes.

"You should talk to his neighbors. One of the kids swapped him booze for meds. Herman had hip, back, elbow, and everything else issues and claimed the booze killed the pain better than the pain-killers. I think he liked to mix them. Anyway, maybe the kid

45

figured pills were worth more than a bottle of Jack Daniels. And check up on the neighbor's dog. I think Herman might have slipped him a pill."

"Or maybe Herman just liked booze and the kid liked to get high. Maybe they swapped technique. But I'll ask about the dog."

"Yeah, maybe. But he had a lot of pills last time I was in the house. You said you didn't see any meds. He was a freakin' pharmacy. Where did it all go?"

Jon grunted. I went inside to hang the keys on the hook and check the board for the next day. Mona posted all the appointments so we could fight over the airport rides. They paid best and usually generated tips.

When I came out, Jon was waiting. "I rented the new Sherlock Holmes movie. We can watch it and make out on the couch."

I smiled. Making out with Jon usually led to better things and I could use some better things right now.

We picked up some take-out tacos on the way home. When we finished the tacos, we started on each other. I'll have to watch that movie sometime.

Over coffee the next morning, I sketched the layout in Herman's living room. I explained how he remembered when to take which pills. I gave as exact a picture as I could about how many and what color and size the various pills were.

"Everything was within reach of his TV chair," I said.

"Anyone else he mention who ran errands for him, supplied him with stuff?"

"No, he mostly used Cool Rides for everything. He told me about the neighbor and the booze when he complained the doctors didn't give him enough pills. But he mentioned slipping one of his precious pills to the neighbor's dog. He was kind of a mean old geezer. He said the booze worked better. If he ran out too soon, the doctor would refuse to give him another scrip. That, and if he ran out on a weekend, he couldn't get any more. So, he probably wouldn't swap them for booze on a Friday night or over the weekend."

"Ok, I got work to do in his neighborhood while I wait for COD." Jon got up from the table. "Come on, I'll give you a ride to work."

He dropped me off and I turned and leaned in the window. "Will they run a tox screen?"

"If I request it."

"Will you?"

"Yeah, I want to know more about what wasn't in his system."

I nodded. "Yeah, more important than what was."

Jon smiled at me and nodded back. "You'd make a good cop."

"Ick," I said and walked into the office.

I didn't get more than two steps into what we euphemistically call the lobby when Mona handed me a fare slip. I groaned. Salvo House. The people who occupy Salvo house are nice enough that I feel almost as guilty taking their money as they are reluctant to part with it. Most of the residents are elderly, some with debilitating illnesses. They hire a cab when public transportation or the senior van can't take care of their travel needs. They never tip, and I don't blame them. I wish the government at some level could afford a van that just went back and forth from the retirement facilities to services and downtown areas.

The upside is that they're always interesting and usually funny even if the conversations lack a certain logic. They've been around for a lot of decades. Their stories date to before cars were the main mode of transport. Today I picked up four ladies that I take to a bicycling/tricycling program for the elderly. They were all born before women had the right to vote. They learned to drive on a Model T and drove an electric car before they were ecologically correct.

"Now those things are back in style. We could have just skipped over the whole gasoline thing and stuck with the electrics. I liked 'em better anyway. Not as noisy," one said to me. "And I read in the paper this morning about how they busted someone for having too much marijuana. It was perfectly legal when I was a kid and I turned out fine. When you get to be my age, you don't give a shit about what other people do. I say let 'em smoke themselves silly."

"I still want to ride a two-wheeler," grumbled the one behind me in the back seat.

"Oh, for heaven's sake. God grant you the power to know when to switch back to a tricycle. You're ninety-two years old."

"If God is granting powers, I'd like the power to have an orgasm with something that isn't plastic," said the middle back seat.

"And I'd like the power to find my pain meds," said the passenger side back seat.

"Don't tell me you've misplaced your oxy again." The conversation traveled back to the middle of the back seat.

I listened to them patter back and forth about life in the fast lane of their nineties and finally dropped

48

them at the bike trail. The front passenger side gave me the ten-dollar fare, and her friends handed me a five-dollar tip.

On my way back to the garage, Mona called and told me to go back to Salvo house. Another senior wanted a ride uptown to do some shopping.

He was waiting outside when I arrived.

"I need to buy a lot of get-well cards. And I just got a new-fangled phone so I can call you when I'm done." He held up a bright red smart phone.

"You know how to use it?"

"Nah, I'll just stop some teenager on the street and ask him how to call you."

I handed him a Cool Rides business card and dropped him uptown. He handed me fifteen dollars.

"Keep the change. I'm loaded right now. But I ain't gonna tip you so good on the trip back. Just so you know." He waved and stomped across the sidewalk.

Driving back, I saw Belle help an elderly man that I recognized from one of the retirement homes out of the cab. I honked and kept going.

Mona called me when I was fifty feet from the garage with another run from Salvo House. The runs were proving to be lucrative. I didn't complain. I pulled up in front of Salvo as Rigger was cramming the last of three walkers into the back of his car. He waved and drove off. I loaded two more walkers, a cane and three gray-haired ladies dressed to the nines into the cab. They were going uptown for lunch. I heard snatches of conversation from the back seat and lots of giggles.

"That young man?...I never use it all anyway... why not have some fun?"

I got back to Cool Rides after returning all the geezers to their various housing situations. Belle and Rigger were right behind me.

"So, did you guys spend the day taking money from little old ladies?" I asked.

"Weird," said Belle. "Good tips from elderly in subsidized housing. They never do that."

"Hey," said Rigger. "Ours not to question why and all that."

"You too?"

"Mona sends us where the action is. The seniors must've got their social security checks."

"Or something," I said and walked into the office. I didn't think any more about the strange day because I was kept busy running a couple of teenagers who had missed the bus and a college student to the train station. I finished up around five thirty. Belle and Rigger had left and the single person on the night crew was driving to the airport. As I handed in my fare money, my personal cell phone buzzed. Jon's number popped up.

"I'm having Chinese tonight. Maybe we can watch Sherlock again."

"I could do Chinese. Did you get spring rolls?"

"I'll stop by in ten." And he clicked off. I could look forward to Jon, Chinese and Sherlock, maybe even in that order.

My new slut shoes were stashed in my oversized bag. They were black faux suede with narrow heels that were about four inches high and little silver bells hanging from the silver bow on the open toe. I had hoped to get a chance to show them to Belle for approval. She told me that the only appropriate place to wear them is where it counts, which, according to her, is the bedroom. I decided to try them out on Jon.

The nice thing about Chinese food is that it is almost as good cold as it is hot.

We were sitting on the sofa, sort of watching the movie in post-coital bliss. I had on Jon's shirt and he had on jeans. I also had on my super shoes. They proved Belle to be a good judge of what's appropriate in the bedroom. No surprise, given her previous profession. I probably couldn't have walked from the living room to the bedroom in them, but since I had been wrapped around Jon and he'd carried me, it didn't matter. He took them off and massaged my foot. I thought nothing could feel better. I was wrong because then he kissed my foot and then he kissed other places and now here we sat, grinning like fools.

"You'd pass Belle's requirements for a taxi driver," Jon said, eyeing my shoes.

"Should I take off the shirt?"

"Be okay with me."

I stood up and unbuttoned it. He pulled me over and kissed my belly button. Then he kissed lower and we were back in the bedroom. I never did see what happened to Sherlock. But it was nice to know that Jon shared Lucille's view's on oral sex.

The next morning, Jon asked me if I had heard anything about Herman from the other drivers.

"No, you hear about cause of death?" I replied.

"Probably today."

"So, what's making you focus on this death? Why wouldn't it be natural?" I asked, thinking that maybe it was just Herman's time.

"I checked the bathroom, the kitchen."

"No meds?"

"No meds."

"You're right, that's all wrong. But anyone could have come in and taken them after he died."

"Yeah, and that's probably where we'll end up. Cause of death will be natural, pills either sold or swapped before he died or stolen after."

"But you'd like to know who, how and why."

"Yeah, I hate loose ends."

"And those meds were probably worth a lot of money on the street."

Jon looked at me. "How do you know about this stuff?"

"I pick up whoever has fare money. They talk, I listen. They usually act as if I'm not there. If there are two of them, they don't know I exist."

"Like who?"

"No one special, just people talking. Rumors about what's going on around town. People like to let other people know they can get stuff. It's nothing you could take into a courtroom."

"Jesus, Honey, courtroom or not, I feel like the taxi drivers know more than the cops in this town. I should interview you every day."

"Should I wear my super shoes?"

Jon grinned. "Come on, I'll give you a ride to work."

I took three people to the liquor store before noon. None of them needed any more booze in their lives.

Two people took screaming cats to the vet. Three mothers and two fathers took screaming children to the doctor's office. I couldn't decide which was worse. At least the cats were caged. Cats and kids were all scary quiet on the way home.

When I got back after delivering the last of them, Willie was standing outside Cool Rides with a tall, elderly man. He had slightly long, bushy white hair and was on the slender side but stood up straight, like he might have been in the military. When I pulled to a stop, he came over to hold the door for me. It was an unexpected and gentlemanly gesture. I just sat there. His blue eyes sparkled, and he offered me his hand. I looked dumbly at the hand, finally figured out what he was doing and grasped it, allowing myself to exit the car with a grace completely foreign to me.

"You must be Honey. Herman told me so much about you. He claimed he couldn't have survived these last few years without Cool Rides."

"Unh?" I replied. The man had to be well into his seventies, but he was still knock-out handsome.

"Honey, this is Sherman Wolenski, Herman's brother." Willie leaned on the car. "Honey? You okay?"

"Uh, yeah. I just didn't expect you this soon." I managed to extract my hand and get out of the car. "You don't look like Herman."

"So I'm told. I'm a few years younger than him." He paused. "Than he was."

As we stood there, Belle pulled up and then Rigger. Belle hopped out and came over to us.

"Hi, I'm Belle." She smiled and swayed her hips. "What modeling agency sent you over and why?"

53

Sherman smiled. Perfect white teeth. Damn. Government-issue dentistry? "I could say the same. Now I've met the two most beautiful cab drivers in the universe."

Willie cleared his throat. "This is Sherman Wolenski, Herman's younger brother. He's here to see to the funeral arrangements."

"Ah," said Belle. "Sorry for your loss."

Rigger came over, introduced himself, shook the offered hand and went inside.

"I'll see you at the funeral, I'm sure," said Belle and followed Rigger. I had a feeling that most of Cool Rides would now be attending Herman's funeral. I would personally introduce Lucille to Sherman. Nobody, including Sherman, seemed to be very sad about Herman's passing.

Then Jon called me with the cause of death.

Chapter Four

"Herman Wolenski died of natural causes. The natural part being that maybe he naturally forgot to take any of the medicine to prevent an embolism from happening."

"That would be the medicine you couldn't find?" I asked.

"None other than...no blood thinners, no pain killers, but like I said, he could have sold it, swapped it, or, hell, even given it away. Nothing that I can arrest anyone for even if I could find them."

"You just can't bust anyone these days."

"No crime, no evidence."

"Bummer. How much of a market could there be for blood thinners?" I grinned. I called Jon a pig when we first met, and I still have residual delight when he can't assert his authority. Hey, we all have issues. "Herman's brother is here to arrange the funeral. He's the opposite of Herman, very nice, very handsome," I added.

"Handsome?"

"Well, for a seventy-something year old. I thought I could introduce him to Lucille. She's going with me to the funeral. She sort of knew Herman."

"Lucille?" Jon said, sounding blank.

"Hello, Jon. What's with the one-word questions? Are you paying attention to me?"

"Yeah, you like Herman's brother and you're going to play match-maker with Lucille. Not a good idea, Honey."

"Lucille loves to meet eligible older gentlemen," I replied.

"I know Lucille. I've known her a long time. She can be very dangerous. He just lost his brother for God's sake. Give him a break."

"She's my date," I answered.

The funeral was the next day. Herman had been cremated and his ashes were scattered on the lake next to the retirement village. I picked up Lucille and met the other drivers and cabs at Cool Rides. The city would be down one taxi company for a few hours. Mona put the phone on vibrate and locked the office. Herman was sent off by a caravan of his favorite taxi company. All five of the colorful cars made for a wonderful parade. Herman would have been happy. Well, maybe not happy but at least interested.

When we arrived, a staff member from the retirement village had a row-boat waiting for Sherman and Herman.

Sherman shook hands with each of us, took the ceramic jar containing Herman and got in the boat. Even Lucille behaved and simply said she was sorry for Sherman's loss.

We all lined up along the shore to bid Herman goodbye. There was an on-shore breeze, which was unfortunate. We walked away, wiping our eyes. We also wiped our clothing, our faces and our hair. Human ash is heavy and gritty, the lake was small, and the breeze was stiff.

Back at the office, Mona put out Lucille's cookies. We turned our phones back to loud and dug in. We were drowning our sorrows in sugar when Jon pulled up in his unmarked. He came in, nodded to Lucille and me and went over to Sherman.

"Mr. Wolenski, I'm police Lieutenant Jon Stevens. I'm handling the investigation into your brother's death. I'm sorry for your loss."

"Thank you. Was there some problem about Herman's passing? I got the coroner's report and it was clearly natural causes." Sherman shook Jon's hand and tried to smile but he looked slightly alarmed at the police presence at his brother's funeral reception.

"No, no questions. The police get involved whenever there's an unattended death."

Sherman nodded. Jon knew he wouldn't get new information. The drugs were gone and there was nothing to connect their absence to Herman's death.

I wandered over to Belle and Rigger. Jon joined us and listened to the chatter about rides—who tipped, who Rigger should or shouldn't pick up, and why or why not.

"Yesterday was not normal," said Belle.

"Yeah, I gathered it was weird somehow," responded Rigger.

"Those geezers never tip. And it wasn't their social security checks. They had money to spend. They were eating uptown, going shopping, having a great time. And most of them tipped. That never happens."

"That's good, isn't it? I mean good for them and good for us? They all seemed happy," said Rigger.

"Yeah, that's what was weird. That group is never that happy and never generous. They gotta worry about how to make it from check to check. They don't eat out and they don't tip," Belle insisted, shaking her four-inch Afro.

Jon listened to this exchange intently, trying not to be noticed. Which is not easy, given his height and looks. But then, Belle is six feet and Rigger is good-looking in a very masculine way.

We pondered the meaning of rich poor people when the Cool Rides phone rang.

"Back to work," said Belle and moved over to where Mona scribbled names and addresses on fare slips.

Jon leaned over and whispered in my ear, "I want to know more about the rich geezers, as Belle calls them. Let's talk tonight over tacos."

"I could do tacos. Maybe we can see the end of Sherlock Holmes."

"Not likely," said Jon.

When I got to Jon's house we settled on the super-sized couch with tacos and watched Sherlock try to look like a woman. Also not easy considering what Robert Downey Jr. looks like.

"So, tell me more about the people who starting tipping yesterday," Jon said, biting into a taco.

"Not much to tell since they reverted to type by today. I took one of them to the doctor because he forgot to order the senior van. He complained about how expensive taxis have gotten and didn't tip. Belle had the same with a lady who needed to get her cat to the vet. She yowled more than the cat."

"Why was your guy going to the doctor?"

"Too much pain. He said they never give out enough painkillers. He wanted more and the doc makes them come in if they use over a certain amount in a week."

"Oxycodone, right?"

"I didn't ask. But whatever the common pain med is for seniors. It's addictive, I guess. They get grumpy if they don't have it. The doctor told this guy he would be socially inappropriate if he didn't take his meds."

"Let me know if you pick him up again or any of the others that were rich for a day."

"You think something's up with the pain meds?"

"No evidence, no crime. But it never hurts to keep your eyes and ears open."

"But you want me to tell you if there's anything I think you should know."

"Just keep me in the loop."

"I'm not a snitch."

"I'm not asking you to be."

"Oh, yeah, you call it a confidential informant. Well, I'm not one of those either." My voice rose as I over-reacted to Jon's questions.

"Honey, we may be talking about something illegal here. Or we may be talking about a bunch of grumpy old folks. Just let me know if you hear anything out of line."

"What's out of line for you isn't always out of line for me. You can follow the law all you want. I follow what I consider to be my own good judgment." I stood up and stomped to the door.

Jon jumped up and got in front of me before I could get out and slam it behind me in a satisfyingly dramatic fashion.

"I just want to know what your own good judgment tells you is going on."

"No, you don't. You want me to spy on some poor people who can barely make it from one social security check to the next. You cops think everyone's guilty of something. It ain't gonna happen until the pig that you are sprouts wings. I'm outta here. Let me know when you learn to fly."

Jon leaned his forehead against the wall and opened the door. I stomped out, my righteous indignation flying like a kite for all to see. Too bad there wasn't anyone besides Jon and me to see it. Then I realized I had no car and no shoes. Belle had dropped me off and my slut shoes and sneakers were on the other side of Jon's door. But I was not about to knock and beg for my shoes. I did have my cell phone. I punched in Belle's number.

"Those shoes work fine but now I can't walk."

"Who is this and why do I care about your shoes?"

"Belle, it's Honey and I just had a fight with that pig who calls himself Lieutenant. He is a smug self-centered idiot and I need a ride home."

"I thought for sure the shoes would solve all your anti-authority problems."

"They did, for one night."

"Maybe we need to do some shopping for the rest of you, like above the knees—a few thongs with holes in the right places."

"There's not enough material in a thong to have a hole anyplace unless you use a paper punch to put it there. And, trust me, Jon would not fit through a paper punch hole. Are you coming to get me?"

Belle sighed. "So good to know. I'll be at the end of the street in five minutes. We want him to think you walked home."

"He has my shoes. He knows I'm not walking home barefoot. And I'm sure he's watching me."

"Whatever, just walk to the end of the street, okay?"

Five minutes later Belle swung around the corner in the cab she had taken home for the night. Drivers do that when they have an early morning run, usually an airport. It's a good way to start the day financially, but a four a.m. run is still hard to enjoy. Belle was already in her sleepers. I felt only slightly guilty about getting her out of bed. She must have been alone because her sleepers were full length, long sleeved and high necked. She was driving in fluffy pink slippers.

"So, what made you pissy with our Lieutenant?"

"He's a pig."

"He's a cop, so that's redundant, but he's still got a great butt. And from the smile on your silly face for the last few days, he has some other fine attributes as well. Like the one that doesn't fit through the paper punch hole?"

I sighed. "Yeah, I didn't know my body could feel that way. I might miss that."

"So, you gonna tell Auntie Belle what the big problem is that would have an otherwise rational woman giving up orgasms like she's never had before?"

"I'm not a snitch."

"I'm not asking you to be. I just thought you might want to vent."

"Not you, Jon. He wants me to keep him informed about the geezer wheezer drug use. I told him when pigs fly. Then I asked if he could fly."

"What did he say?"

"He opened the door for me."

"Uh oh. That's not a good sign for the future of your sex life."

"Don't worry about my sex life. I'm worried about those seniors." I slouched down, strangling myself with the seatbelt. I sat back up. "I mean, some of them are pretty nice people. And what if something is going on? You think I want to see a bunch of grandmas in the slammer?"

Belle's mouth twitched. She almost smiled.

"And then there's that kid, who apparently has left the hospital for who knows where. What if he goes stupid and tries too many pills again?"

I had told Belle about the kid. I hadn't told Jon. It wasn't my job to make sure the police communicated with each other. I had called the hospital earlier that day and the kid was gone.

"It ain't your problem, Honey. Keep your nose out of it. If something illegal really is happening, the cops will find out about it sooner or later. Your job is to drive."

"So, with or without me, Jon will work it out?"

"Yup."

"But what if Herman died because someone stole his meds?"

"Why wouldn't he just ask the doc for more?"

"You had to know Herman. He'd refuse to take meds just to be defiant sometimes. He was pretty good about the blood pressure meds because he knew he could die without 'em, real quick. But if someone swiped his mini pharmacy, he might not be able to replace it fast enough. Or he might not try. Or he might mean to and then forget. If they took everything and all the paper with days of the week on it, he might just forget the whole thing."

"Sounds like he needed one of those personal care attendants. It's a regular position in most retirement villages. PCA is a pretty good job. I checked it out when I moved down here. Before I decided to continue my self-employment situation."

"He went through five of them. Count it on your hand, five."

"Huh. Service jobs are tough. I should know. What'd he complain about?"

"Everything from sexual molestation to grand theft auto. And he didn't have a car." I told her about his comments when I tried to fasten his seatbelt. "He claimed they stole his meds, his TV remote, his bottled water, keys to the car he didn't have. Anything that he misplaced, they stole. The retirement management was about ready to give up."

"He had a lot of mean in him."

"Yeah, it's weird how different his brother is from him."

"You introduce Sherman to Lucille?" asked Belle.

"Just at the service. I thought if she wanted to see him, she could invite him to something at the senior center. Or maybe on a gun shooting date."

"You're kidding. She goes on bang-up dates?"

"She got a special girly gun just for the occasion," I said with a grin.

"She is such a hot ticket. Go girl, I say."

"Maybe I'll talk to her about the drugs thing."

"Just remember, Jon is her landlord. They're pretty close," Belle said with a frown.

"Yeah, but she has an attitude about him. I haven't figured it out completely yet. She feels free to pass judgment and tell him when she disagrees with him. Besides, she thinks I'm good for him."

"Humph. Just don't do anything stupid." Belle slapped her forehead as we pulled up in front of my apartment. "Oh, I forgot, I'm talking about you."

"Geez, thanks for the ride and thanks for all the support." I got out of the car and closed the door. "Love the slippers."

Belle leaned over the seat.

"Honey?"

I leaned down to the window. "Yeah?"

"Just be careful. I hate to say it about a cop, but Jon's honest and he seems to mean well. You don't have to be a snitch to tell him when someone needs help."

"Yeah, I guess." I shrugged and went inside. Too many decisions, too much information. I hoped there was something stupid to watch on my mini TV. I already missed Jon's big screen.

Belle was right. I had no idea how to gauge when someone needed help, much less get it for them without causing trouble. I decided to focus on driving and try to stay off Jon's radar. How stupid was that?

Chapter Five

It turned out that my withdrawal from Jon's big screen was too much and I couldn't watch anything, stupid or not, on my tiny TV. Janet Evanovich and my e-reader kept me up way too late. I could really identify with Stephanie Plum. I seemed to be just as much of a klutz when it came to romance.

I staggered out of bed the next morning and stood under the shower until I resembled a prune. But at least I was an awake prune. Dressed in my usual black jeans, white tee and sneakers, I headed toward my favorite latte shop. We don't have ordinary coffee shops in Northampton. Each one tries to outdo the next in terms of strength, toppings, and additions to the basic cup. I stopped at Coffee AM and got the basic salted caramel extra-large skinny mocha with whip and a shot of peppermint. Simple, with enough calories to last until the world ends. Or at least until lunch.

I walked from there to Cool Rides.

When I got there, Belle had returned from her early run and gone out to pick up the Judge from his mother's house. According to Mona, Belle had accepted the Judge's invitation to coffee. Five minutes after I arrived, she drove in. She was learning to dress down a little bit from her days as a ho. She wore black pants and a black sleeveless top. The top had enough sparkle to blind the space station and it was cut low enough to distract the astronauts with her cleavage.

"So, when's the date?"

"What date?"

"Don't be like that. The Judge."

"It's just coffee. Definitely not a date." But her Mona Lisa expression betrayed her.

"Okay, spill. Why the smiley face?"

Belle giggled and clapped a hand over her mouth.

I stared at her and said, "I can't believe you just giggled. He did something when you picked him up. He did, didn't he? What?"

"The man can kiss, man, can the man kiss! Who'd have thought such a straight and sober-as-a-judge guy could do that? I have some experience in that area, not with clients mind you. But I'm no novice."

I fisted my hands over my head and danced in a little circle. "Yes, yes, yes," I sang.

"What are you excited about? He didn't kiss you."

"Yeah, but you're my best friend. I can live vicariously, right?"

"I'm your best friend? I don't think I've ever had a best friend." Belle looked a little perplexed, unsure of her ground with such an earth-shaking pronouncement from me.

"Hey, girlfriend, I'm not asking you to die for me but we stick together. Especially in the man department," I said.

"Yeah, how's it going with Lieutenant Stud? And why do you need vicarious living?" She looked at me suspiciously.

"I need to figure out how to get my super shoes back."

"Don't hold your breath too long," said Belle and nodded to the far end of the parking lot.

Jon was walking in our direction. Dangling from the tips of his fingers was a pair of black shoes with silver bells. My shoes.

I put my fists on my hips and glowered, trying for angry.

"Be nice," said Belle as she walked toward the office. I gave her the one-finger salute behind my back.

The angry thing didn't work longer than it took Jon to run a finger down the side of my face, turn his baby blue eyes on me and say, "I hear these work really well in the right places."

"Yeah, what happened to being a snitch?"

"Honey, you do your job, and I'll do mine. I won't have a problem with yours if you don't have one with mine. And neither job belongs where these shoes belong."

"Just don't try to mix them up."

Jon just smiled. Then he kissed the tip of my nose, leaned his forehead on mine and kissed more of me. My focus fuzzed a little, then it disappeared completely.

Mona came out of the office just as Jon's hand was going where it wasn't allowed in public.

"Honey, you're up."

"I'm not the only one," I mumbled.

Jon grinned. "Time for work." He handed me the shoes, which of course caught Mona's attention.

"Whoa, don't drive in those! Where did you get them and do they come in my size?" she asked, handing me a fare slip.

She disappeared back inside before I could say "slut shoe." I stashed the shoes in my oversized bag and briefly contemplated Mona's need for slut shoes. She usually dressed in sneakers for work. She needed to be able to stand up for long periods and to move around quickly when necessary. Sometimes she helped wash cars so she couldn't be in anything too dressy. I had never actually seen her in anything sexier than Nikes.

I looked at the fare slip and smiled. Meri Edemson's cat needed a ride to the vet. I would drop it off and do Meri's grocery shopping while the cat got tested for everything a twenty-year old cat could have wrong with it, which was everything. Meri was a cherished fare because she insisted on tipping like the end of the world was at hand and Cool Rides was the only way out of Armageddon. She was the only customer I had ever told not to tip excessively. Her response was that she had lots of money, no relatives, and what would she do with it when she died? When I got to her apartment, Meri had Miss Kitty in her carrier and was cooing reassuring words through the wire door. Miss Kitty knew better and had a wide-eyed look of complete distrust.

She hissed and spat in anger when I picked up the case.

The vet's office was the usual chaos of creatures under stress. The resident cat, a huge black male named Bad, sat on the counter blinking his green eyes, undisturbed by the bedlam, tail twitching occasionally. A Great Dane was pressed as close to its owner as possible. The dog whined. It put one huge paw on its person's lap and looked ready to add the rest of its body. A cat carrier on the lap of the lady next to the Dane had a paw sticking out the air holes, waving its claws and looking for blood. Growling, screeching, barking and a pitiful yowling filled the air. I shoved my cat carrier at the vet's assistant and fled to the grocery store. Now I understood the need for kitty Prozac. If everyone slipped a pill to their animal before a vet visit, it might drop the stress level down far enough that the vet's assistant wouldn't need her own Prozac by the end of the day.

Since my experience with Herman, I noticed medications more. There was a massive, locked, glass-fronted case in the vet's office filled with boxes, vials and bags of animal medication. I wondered how many doggy tranquilizers would make an average-sized human high enough to not care…about anything.

I parked at the mega-grocery store and looked at Meri's list of absolute needs and then her list of "if you can find it, I'd like one." She listed bottled water under "must have" and a specific brand under "if you can find it." I once figured water is water, but Meri had disabused me of that point of view. Twenty different kinds of canned cat food, the little tiny cans, were on the list. Miss Kitty didn't like to eat the same food more than once a month so that was under "must have." There was a series of obscure kinds of soups on her wish side of the list, as was bacon. Since the retirement home had permanently turned off her stove after she almost burned the building down, I skipped the soup and bacon. Technically, she could microwave those, but she hadn't figured out that appliance yet. Four different kinds of aspirin to cure four different problems, some stomach calming liquid, something to

69

make her joints function more smoothly, her nose run less, her eyes look clear and, finally, a breath freshening, tooth whitening, plaque removing, enamel hardening toothpaste were all on her "must have" list. I found them all easily. It was scary how many ways Madison Avenue had convinced us we needed to take care of ourselves.

When I got back to Meri's apartment, I had six bags of groceries and a cat carrier with a very unhappy Miss Kitty telling the universe what a horrible person I was. I staggered through Meri's door and found her sitting in the chair by the door wearing her coat and hat and an unhappy face.

"I need to go to the doctor," she said, fighting tears. "I know I took the right pill on the right day and he won't believe me." She sniffled. "Now I don't have enough pills and he won't give me any more until I come see him. I'm not losing my mind." A big tear ran down her cheek. "I just can't be," she whispered.

I sat next to her. "I'll call Mona and see if I can run you to the doctor's office. I don't think I have anything else right now."

Mona told me to go ahead and I offered Meri my arm. We let Miss Kitty out of the cage. She hissed and zipped under the bed. Gathering all the medications that Meri was taking, we headed out the door.

"How do you make sure you take the right pill on the right day?" I asked her.

"I have one of those boxes with all the compartments in it. But I have to remember to put the pills in the compartments and I can't read the printing because they make it too small. I'm sure I put the pills in, but some of them are missing. All the pain killers are gone."

"Is anything else missing?"

"I don't think so, but the doctor keeps track of what I'm taking, so he'll know."

The doctor finally agreed to give Meri another prescription for painkillers and a new compartmentalized box with the days of the week in extra-large printing. When we got back to her apartment, we divided the pills into compartments together. I sat with her for a while just because she seemed to need it. After ten minutes, Miss Kitty came out and curled up next to her. When I left, the two of them were sitting on the couch watching the Animal Channel. There was a small rodent running back and forth on the TV screen and both human and cat head tracked the action back and forth like a tennis match. I closed the door quietly.

When I got back to the office it was afternoon. Belle had run three people to the dentist, two to a lunch meeting, four to an early movie, five separate trips from a cheap motel/rooming house outside town and one "scene of an accident" to the tow lot. I still made more money in tips than she did. She had also squeezed the coffee date with the judge in there somehow. That required a gossip session that even Mona wanted to attend.

"So, spill. What's he like?"

"Carlton? Local university and Tulane Law in New Orleans."

"I know where Tulane is. But what's he like?"

"He's nice, interesting and made me laugh a lot." Belle was ignoring our curiosity.

"So, when's the next date?"

"Nope."

"What, nope?"

"Ain't gonna happen. Get over it."

"What is wrong with you?" I said.

"Wrong with me?" Our voices were getting loud.

"Yeah, he's nice, he's smart, funny and hot. What do you want in a guy?" I said.

"Maybe I like white, maybe I like women, maybe I like white women. Maybe he likes white women. What the hell business is it of yours?" Belle turned to Mona. "I need a ride." She charged toward the office.

"He asked you out, not some white woman," I yelled after her and realized that I was a white woman. I never thought about my race much. A lot of our clients were in the lower economic strata because that's who can't afford to have a car. So, I was more attuned to socio-economic class than to race. Belle didn't flaunt her economic class, which was way better than mine, or her race. And for that, she was an even better best friend. I let her go, knowing this would blow over. I was determined to keep my BFF even if that meant keeping my nose out of her other relationships.

Mona stomped back into the office after Belle. Seconds later Belle stormed out, hopped in a car and drove off. I dragged my feet into Mona's lair.

"So, where did you send her?"

"Couple of teenagers needed a ride home from downtown. She'll be fine. Let her cool down. She's not used to people caring about her."

"Maybe we are being too nosy."

"Or maybe we just have her best interests at heart."

I looked at Mona. "Not me. I'm just a snoop. You got anything for me?"

"Nope, but as long as we're just snoops, let's just snoop." Mona booted up her computer and googled the judge.

"Whoa, what's this?" I leaned closer. I had forgotten that Mona had some pretty deep computer programs. Programs that allowed her to do her own background checks on potential drivers. The police ran a check, called a CORI, on all drivers who applied for a position. They could find out if anyone was a serial killer, child molester, flasher or anything else they considered dangerous to the public. Although there were several women I knew, such as Lucille, who might enjoy a flasher. Probably a few men too. But Mona could go deeper. She could find out what kind of toothpaste someone used if she needed to know.

As her computer ran through the Judge's college and law school years, an interesting series of photos popped up. They were blurry but recognizable and I didn't know what technology took them. It might have been a cell phone, but I didn't remember when those made their first appearance. But they had been posted on Facebook. The first was the front of Naked Ladies Bar and Grill. Then it looked like the photographer went inside, using a flash. There was a young Judge Witherspoon leaning against a pole bare-chested and mostly bare everything else. Yummm. The caption read "It's a living." Belle wasn't the only one who had worked her way through college.

Mona and I were contemplating the possibilities when Rigger drove up. He had been running short hauls from the Survival Center to all over town. The Survival Center distributes free food, clothing and shoes to anyone in need. It has a transportation fund for someone who finds themselves with three children and twenty sacks of groceries and a long walk home. Cool Rides provides an alternative. And we have air-conditioned cars.

Rigger got out and came into the office. He was wearing a black tee shirt that said MY PHONE IS SMARTER THAN ME on it.

"Cute tee shirt," I said.

"Yeah, I got one that says MY PHONE CAN BEAT UP YOUR PHONE." The threat of a new generation of kindergarteners.

Mona smiled. "Used to say my brother is bigger than yours. I guess the cell phone has replaced a lot of stuff."

Riggs leaned over Mona's shoulder to check out what we were checking out.

"Whoa, yummm," he said. "Who is it?"

"Someone we're trying to fix Belle up with. She's not going for it."

"That's the judge? Holy shit! Are we sure he's straight?"

"Oh, yeah."

"Oh, bummer," said Riggs.

I looked at him. "I thought you were otherwise engaged. That's why you moved here."

"Hey, a man needs some fantasy life too. You telling me you don't look at anyone besides the lieutenant?"

Mona looked over at Riggs. "She looked you over real careful when you got the job."

Riggs beamed. "I'm flattered."

I smirked. "Tell Belle the Judge is the new man of your dreams. Jealousy can be a strong motivator. Maybe it'll get her pointed in the right direction."

"What direction would that be?" Riggs asked.

"Hey, come on. He's smart, handsome, and there's a spark there. I've seen it with my own eyes."

"What's her problem?"

"She's uptight about her previous profession."

Riggs pointed at the computer. "Apparently she doesn't know about his previous profession."

"Maybe not, but his profession wasn't illegal. I'm pretty sure hers was."

"All she has to do is tell him. If he backs off, he's a jerk and she's well rid of him," said Riggs.

"And if he doesn't and she's still not sure?"

"Let him be a friend." Riggs looked back at the car. "Wait a minute. I have just the tee shirt for her." He trotted out the door to the car. When he came back in he spread out a black tee shirt on Mona's desk. It said LIFE IS A BUMPY ROAD, FRIENDS ARE THE SHOCK ABSORBERS.

"Aw," said Mona. "That's so sweet it's sickening."

"What's with you and the tee shirts?" I asked, looking at Riggs.

"I'm thinking about starting a tee shirt company. Market them in stores in the area."

We were brainstorming all the cute, politically correct and politically incorrect sayings we could suggest for Riggs' tee shirt company when Belle drove up, got out of the car and came inside.

"Did you know where those kids lived?" She squeezed into Mona's tiny office and frowned.

"Florence Heights." With four of us crowding around the computer, it was a tight squeeze. I hoped Belle didn't get hissy with Mona.

"Uh huh. Right next door to Mrs. Witherspoon."

"Oh yeah? The Judge's mother? I didn't know that. She say hi?"

"No, but he did."

"Nice, he was visiting his mother."

"No, his mother wasn't there. He was weeding her garden. He was on his goddamn knees weeding her garden." She narrowed her eyes at Mona. "Without his shirt."

Riggs looked at Belle. "As good as I'm thinking?"

"Oh yeah. Maybe better. And you're not supposed to be thinking about that at all." Belle leaned over the desk. "What's the tee shirt? New idea?" Apparently Belle already knew about Riggs' idea for a tee shirt company.

"That's for you. In case the Judge just wants to be friends."

"Great. I'll wear it on our next date."

I looked at Belle. "He asked you out again and you said yes?"

"Yeah, we could be friends, too. We have a lot in common." She looked over the shirt at Mona's computer. "What's that?"

Mona went to hit the close button, but Belle beat her to it and grabbed her hand.

"Just some research that Honey and I were doing." I noticed she emphasized my name and put it first.

Riggs stepped forward. "Maybe she should see this. Good to know what a man looks like under the best of circumstances."

Belle looked at the screen. "That's Carlton. Holy shit! That's Carlton when he was stripping." She sat down in front of the computer. "He should get that one framed. He looks great. He still looks good, but he has put on a few pounds."

"A woman after my own heart," said Riggs.

"He says he doesn't have time to exercise. I told him you gotta make time."

"Still after my own heart."

"Wait a minute," said Mona, glancing over at me. "You know about his stripping?"

"Well, duh. He told me when we went out for coffee."

"And what did you tell him?" I asked.

"I said I had a similar experience working my way through college."

"And?"

"And we got distracted talking about our college experiences. Then he asked me what it was like, being a prostitute. I just about fell off my chair."

"He knew?"

"Yeah, word gets around the courthouse grapevine pretty fast. He knew before he asked me out. But," she shook her finger at me, "I didn't know that he knew and he knew that."

"So, he knew your employment history, but he knew that you didn't know that he knew. And then he told you about his employment which you didn't know about and he knew that you didn't know. Advantage to the Judge." I grinned.

"Okay, enough," said Mona. "We're running a cab company here, not a gossip column. Riggs, you got a train pick-up. They just called from Hartford, so get going. Belle and Honey, you have Virginia Percy in forty-five minutes to the airport. Honey, you're on special assistance detail; Miss Virginia asked for you." Special assistance means one person to stay with the car and one person to help the client snag a wheelchair and get through security.

"Huh," said Belle. "I can do special just as well."

"Yeah, but Virginia likes your driving. She said you have flair. I didn't ask for elaboration. Now, out! I got paperwork to do."

Miss Virginia, as she preferred being called, was another favorite of the drivers. She is a proper Southern lady with a backbone of steel. Her voice is soft with just enough accent to let you know she hails from south of the Mason-Dixon line. Everyone behaves in her presence. She graduated from Smith College and decided she liked small town living, so she stayed. She always seems larger than life to me and it took me three months to realize she is only 5'2" tall. I would love to see a "who's in charge here" play-off between her and Lieutenant Jon. But she is also in her eighties or some age over social security. A gentlewoman never reveals her age, so we aren't sure where in her eighties she really is but she does have some physical issues. Thus, the need for a wheelchair and some assistance at the airport.

Belle and I adjourned to the lounge and flopped onto the overstuffed sofa.

"You never told me about why you did the prostitute thing."

"You never asked. Why'd you decide to drop out of college and hitchhike across the country? I think my work was safer than your play."

I thought about that for a second. "So, I hitched across the country because it was cheaper than a bus, faster and better company. I didn't have any money and I was not, not going to ask my parents for any." Although I knew damn well they would have given me a bus ticket to anywhere. "I wanted to meet people."

"Which you could have done on a bus."

"How did we end up talking about me? I want to know why you decided to work as a prostitute instead of, say, wait tables in a good restaurant. You can make pretty good tips doing that."

"Honey, that couldn't match what I was making." She smiled a "you know this" smile. "And I wasn't in a huge city where you need a pimp, a lookout or bail money. That's a lot of overhead. When I was in Maine, I was in control and the money went in my pocket. There were three of us and it worked out pretty well. Until the other two decided to get married. That was the end of that arrangement. I invested a pile of money in, among other things, a fruit company. I figured everyone eats apples, right? That was a few years ago when Apple was cheaper. Now it helps pay for the shoe supply. I knew I needed to move. I threw a dart at the map and hit Springfield, Massachusetts. Not a big city, but there was overhead and already an infrastructure that I had to fit into. That's where my stupid husband came into it. He pimped for me. Most of the profits went to his habits or to his bosses. Lucky for me, he didn't know about my investments. But I lost all the control over the business, so I was ready to quit when the old man was murdered. And here we are."

I didn't ask if she really married the old man and why. We didn't have time for that story. I had more questions, like what Belle did with those two-inch fingernails, but Mona called from the office, "Time to get your asses in gear. The car too."

Belle and I hot-footed it out the door. We pulled up in front of Miss Virginia's single-story house ten minutes later. It was on a quiet street and painted a soft moss green with bright red trim around the windows and door. If Hansel and Gretel had visited a good witch instead of almost getting their asses cooked, this is what her house in the forest would have looked like. Flowers in brightly painted pots adorned the steps. The painted pots were color coordinated with the flowers. Miss Virginia had an emerald thumb.

Three suitcases were stacked on what Miss Virginia would call the veranda. There was no sign of her, which was odd because she was usually ready at least a half hour ahead and would sit on the conveniently placed plastic chair until we arrived. She was never late.

"Safety check," Belle and I said in unison. Miss Virginia Percy was one of our customers who had given us a key to her house and told us to check on her if she failed to be outside waiting when we were there to pick her up. With the elderly, this is not unusual. If there isn't a family member close by, they frequently like to know someone will find their body before it becomes too gross for the funeral home to make it more beautiful than it ever was in life. Since we had contact with Miss V at least once a week, we were the designated grossness preventers.

"I'll get her, you load up the luggage. She probably just went inside for one last visit to the bathroom." Another common problem for the elderly. I couldn't wait to gain the wisdom of age.

I started up the walk. Belle got out and opened the hatchback. I reached the first step. The door to the house was ajar. I put my finger against it and nudged. As it drifted open, I could see completely through the shotgun style house to the back door. Presumably, one could fire a shotgun in the front door and hit someone in the back yard. A small powder room was off to the left side. The back door exited the kitchen onto a stone patio. Miss Virginia stood in front of the bathroom door. She wore a flower print dress and her traveling shoes and clutched her pocketbook to her chest.

I could see the reason she wasn't waiting for us. A short, scrawny man had a gun pointed at her chest and was too close to miss. His hand shook so badly he could barely support the weapon. He hadn't seen me. I backed up a step and found my cell phone in my pocket. I was dialing 911 when six feet of sparkling black streaked by me. Belle hit the home invader mid-section and kept going. The gun flew out of his hand, bounced under the couch and shot the cushion. They careened through the living room, dining room, kitchen and out the back door with the guy flipped over Belle's shoulder—arms waving, eyes wide in panic and shock. Belle grabbed the doorframe as she passed it and ducked. She stopped, her burden didn't. He flew off her shoulder, crashed to the stone and lay still. I finished dialing and babbled the address to the dispatcher.

"Duct tape!" Belle yelled.

I grabbed it out of her purse which was lying by Miss Virginia's luggage and rushed over to the now-groaning body. I managed to finish taping his wrists and ankles by the time I heard the sirens. Belle collapsed in one of the patio chairs. I leaned over the idiot. He was starting to move. Feet thumped in the front hallway. The cavalry had arrived.

"If you can't fix it with duct tape, it ain't worth the effort," said Belle.

"I think I might need to reschedule my flight," said Miss Virginia.

"What the fuck?" said Jon as the sirens died down behind him.

Chapter Six

"Uh, oh," I said.

Jon holstered his weapon. His face was in cop mode with a hint of exasperation. He stared at me as he took in the situation. I was pretty sure even my slut shoes wouldn't brighten his mood. If I was wearing them, which I wasn't. Belle was the only one of us who could actually drive in that kind of shoe.

He motioned to one of the uniforms. Two of them went into the bedrooms, one went through into the back yard.

"Clear!" I heard echo from all sources.

"So, who wants to tell me who this guy is and why he's tied up like a pig going to the slaughter house?" Jon's laser blue eyes settled on me.

"I didn't do…" I squeaked.

"I think they may have saved my life," Miss Virginia spoke up.

"Damn right," said Belle.

"I want a lawyer," said the taped-up pig.

My vocal cords weren't exactly paralyzed but they weren't loose and happy either.

"Okay," Jon sighed. "I'm going to take a short statement about all this from the three of you. Then I'll take our friend here down to the station and expect to see all of you there before the end of my shift today."

"Young man," began Miss Virginia, "I have a flight to catch."

"And since you already caught my perp, I have some witnesses to interview. Now or later. Take your pick. As of right now, I'm free all day."

Miss Virginia turned to the telephone. "I will call my travel agent and have her reschedule my flight for tomorrow. I shall expect a ride to the station house and back after the interview. I have no intention of allowing this horrible, foolish young man to ruin my trip."

"Good plan. Honey? Belle? Care to join us?"

Belle shrugged her shoulders and gave Jon a look. "I'll call Mona and see what's booked. If we happen to be free, we can all drag our heroic asses down to the copper shack and give the man his interview," she said. Belle had dozens of names for the new police station and she grinned as she made the phone call.

Jon turned back to me. "I'll meet all of you at the station. You can make it there without creating any more mayhem, right?"

"I didn't do this!" I huffed indignantly. I pointed to the home invader who was being shoved into one of the blue and whites. "That guy is an idiot. And his gun is under the sofa, in case you're interested."

"The crime scene guys will be here shortly, but I appreciate the tip." He wasn't about to get on his hands and knees to retrieve it with three ladies watching his very fine rear end. "Why don't you and Belle help Miss Virginia into the taxi and get going? I'll be right behind you."

We caravanned to the police station. The cruiser with the intruder led with our taxi containing me, Belle and Miss Virginia next, and Jon in his crappy-looking unmarked bringing up the rear. When we got to the station, Jon came over and graciously offered Miss Virginia his hand. She insisted on staying in the car until he arrived to help her out. She once explained to me that she expected the male of the species to open doors for her. Adding that if women raised their expectations, men had better rise to meet them. Belle slammed the door inches from Jon's fingers. He would give her grief for not waiting for the police when there was a loaded weapon involved. He considered her actions foolish; she considered them heroic. And he knew I never passed up a good use of duct tape.

We walked into the clean, uncluttered new space. It would stay that way for maybe weeks or even days. It would be that place where every cop wanted to work. Then reality would conquer newness and the smell of unwashed bodies would conquer fresh air.

Jon showed the three of us into an interrogation room. Normally we would be separated but Miss Virginia was gripping both of us with an intensity that intimidated even Jon. When he tried to escort us in different directions, she simply stared at him like he was a naughty five-year old.

I remember a teacher in grade school with that look. No one, not even the class clown, defied her.

Jon held the chair for Miss V. Belle and I were left to seat ourselves. I settled in next to Miss Virginia. Belle was still busy putting some effort into pushing Jon's buttons. She walked around the perimeter of the small space, pausing at the one-way window. When she got up close, she pulled out a lipstick and used the window to apply a thick layer to her full lips. She smiled at the image, took a step closer and planted a full mouth smooch on the blackened glass. She backed up to admire the imprint. It was pretty luscious.

"Oh, for Christ's sake, Belle, sit down." Jon finally pulled out a chair for her, across the table from Miss Virginia and me. It was easier than letting her play "who can piss on the other guy's shoes?" She sauntered over, curtsied, and planted herself delicately on the hard metal seat. Jon, his expression unreadable, took a seat at the head of the table. I've read that if a table is rectangular, the seat of power is at the long end, facing the door. That's why negotiating tables are always round. Jon sat in the coveted power seat.

"Lieutenant, where is my attacker?" Score one for Miss Virginia. She got out the first question, but Jon wasn't about to yield control.

"He's in custody. The EMT decided not to send him to the hospital." He gave Belle a withering look. She responded with a huge grin.

"I wanted to talk to you before I question him." Jon directed this to Miss V.

"Very well then, I feel quite safe now. Honey and Belle provide me with comfort."

The implication was not lost on Jon. The two women sitting with her were more important to Miss V than being in a police station, no matter how new, pristine and wonderful to work in.

He grimaced and dove in. "Were you in the house when the intruder entered?"

"Yes, I had put my luggage out on the porch. I then returned to the powder room." Miss Virginia held her head up but didn't look at Jon, the only male in the room, when she admitted to actually urinating.

"Do you know how he came in?"

"Well, he walked in of course."

Jon looked down at his hands. They gripped the pencil harder. "Which point of entry did he use? The front door, following you, or the back? A window?"

"I have no earthly idea. When I came out of the bathroom, he was standing in the hallway. He was very surprised to see me. Which means, I guess, that he didn't follow me in. Perhaps he was in there when I took my unfortunate break but I didn't see him until I came out of the ladies' room." She blinked and focused on a spot on the wall. I suspected the shock of the situation was beginning to settle in.

"Did he speak to you?"

"Oh, yes." Her gaze moved to her hands. She sat silently.

"Miss Virginia?"

"Yes?"

"What did he say?"

"Oh."

Jon waited.

"Well, first he jumped back as if he was startled to see me. Then he pulled a large weapon from the back of his pants." A tear ran down her cheek.

Belle suddenly stood, picked up her chair and moved it to the other side of the table. Miss V was now flanked by both of us.

Jon smiled slightly, appearing to understand the solidarity of the womanhood. "Good idea," he said, moving out of the seat at the head of the table and sitting opposite us. He could now easily look at each one of us, or all of us at once. Position of power back to Jon.

"Did he say anything to you?" he repeated.

Belle and I continued to look at Jon.

"My goodness, yes."

"What did he say?"

"Well, he asked me where it was. I had no idea what he was talking about. I remained silent. Sometimes that's the best policy."

Jon and Miss V went back and forth for another half hour. She was starting to look too tired to keep going. Jon suggested she go home. He would visit her in the morning. He asked me to come back after I had delivered her home. He told Belle to stay put.

She pushed her chair back, slipped off her shoes and put her feet up on the desk.

Jon escorted Miss V to the door. I trailed behind.

When we got to the front entrance, Miss V sat down heavily in one of the waiting chairs.

Jon pulled me aside. "Get her settled and come back here right away." His blue eyes nailed me to the floor. "I mean right away, Honey."

"She might still be in danger. I should stay with her," I mumbled.

"I have a cruiser that will follow you to her house and stay there. I'll have them take shifts watching the house until she's gone to visit her kids."

"Oh well, okay. I guess that should keep her safe enough."

I was turning around to help Miss V to her feet when Lucille burst through the front door like Rambo ready to take on all comers. She spotted Virginia and made a beeline for her, arms open with the look of a mother hen facing down a fox. "Oh, Ginny, what happened?"

Miss Virginia fell into Lucille's arms.

I glanced outside and saw Riggs leaning against a Cool Rides car, which accounted for how Lucille had gotten here so quickly. Word spreads fast in the senior community. Both Lucille and Virginia used the senior center for a variety of purposes. I thought about that for a few seconds and then it hit me.

So did Herman Wolenski. So did Meri Edmenson. Most of the Cool Rides senior clients used the center. Sooner or later, we all would use it. That is if it, we, and the planet lasted long enough. I was pretty sure the planet would last, but the senior center might be beachfront property from what the climate news bloggers said. Right now, I needed to get Miss V and Lucille to their respective residences and drag my ass back to the police station.

Lucille guided Miss V down the steps. "Ginny is going to spend the night at my house," she announced. "Riggs can take us to her house to pick up the baggage. Someone will call Mona about when Ginny will be going to the airport."

That left me at the police station. I trudged back to the interrogation room. Belle was still sitting with her feet up on the table, playing with her cell phone. Jon was nowhere in sight. I updated Belle on who was going where and that Lucille had things under control.

"You can always count on Lucille," Belle said without looking up from her phone.

I harrumphed and sat down. "So, where's Jon?"

"I am not my brother's keeper and the Lieutenant isn't a brother in my language anyway. I got no idea where he went. I'm just following orders, but if he don't drag his sorry but pretty tush in here soon, I got other things to occupy my time."

89

I'd always admired Belle's willingness to defy Jon. She was better at it than I was. "Me too," I mumbled.

Five minutes later, Jon came through the door. His tie was gone, and his shirt sleeves were rolled up. His hair was spiked up from running hands of frustration through it. He looked way too sexy. "Okay," he sighed. "Let's have your version of what happened."

Belle told him about her courageous, life-saving tackle of the idiot invader. I told him about making a phone call to 911. Other than that, we didn't have much to offer. We knew the intruder had a gun, but Jon knew that because the police had the weapon. He took a few notes. After an hour of going over timelines, minute by minute, we all gave up. Jon tossed his pencil down.

He stood up and we all trooped out. Belle and I started for the exit.

"Honey?" Jon was behind me.

"What?" I was talked out and more than a little grumpy.

Jon came closer. His eyes were somehow softer. "Come over tonight. There's a ball game on the big screen. You can have the controls."

"Ummm," I hummed noncommittally and followed Belle out.

It was close to the end of my shift and past the end of Belle's. We decided to stop for a burger. Belle could drop me off at Jon's after that. I figured Jon would be at Lucille's side of his house, talking to Miss Virginia, and I could get dessert there.

We finished eating and took the cab back to Cool Rides. Belle swapped it in for her Mini Cooper. I knew enough about Belle's finances to know she had invested well. She had enough spare dough to get a car which was more than I had. I took advantage of her willingness to transport. We zipped out of the parking lot and wove through downtown traffic and pedestrians. The Cooper handled like a barrel racer and we were at Jon's house in less than five minutes.

I hopped out and Belle took off down the street like she was headed for the Indy 500. Jon was leaning against the door jamb of Lucille's side of the large Victorian, his arms crossed over his chest.

"Tell me she doesn't drive like that in the taxi." He pushed off the door, standing aside to let me in.

"She saw you. Otherwise she drives pretty slow and sedate."

Jon grunted, followed me in and closed the door. I was right about dessert. The smell of fresh baking hit and my brain stopped functioning on any level above that of a predator. The prey was chocolate, chocolate chunk. I snatched the unlucky cookie.

Miss Virginia nibbled a sugar cookie. She looked better than she had a few hours ago. Lucille's cookies had restorative powers. I'd also bet Jon was getting more information under easier circumstances. Miss V did not look like she was suffering in his presence. Actually, she looked like she was enjoying his attention. Jon did know how to charm.

"I think he was about to come into the bathroom when I opened the door. He seemed very startled." Miss V took another nibble of her cookie.

"What did he say when he saw you?" asked Jon.

"Oh, I wouldn't repeat that word in this company."

Jon looked at me and Lucille. "In the interest of accuracy, I don't think this company would object."

"Shit," said Miss Virginia. "That's what he said."

"Ah," said Jon and lifted a cookie off the plate.

"Then he pulled out a very large weapon and waved it around and asked where the shit was." She paused. "I didn't know what he meant. I just stared at him."

"Did he say anything else?"

"Well, he didn't have time. Belle used her superior powers at that moment. I really do believe she is a Wonder Woman in her own way. A very good driver also, I might add."

Jon didn't reply. He clearly disagreed with Miss V's comparison of Belle to Wonder Woman.

"What do you keep in the bathroom that he might have been interested in?" Jon asked, choosing to ignore any comments related to Belle's behavior.

Miss V. turned a light shade of pink. "Most of what's in there are women's things. Perhaps he wanted to use the facilities."

"Miss Virginia, where do you keep your medications?"

"Oh, well, if he had a headache, perhaps he was after some aspirin, although I don't use it very often myself. It disagrees with me. I find one replaces the headache with a stomach ache."

"What about any prescription medicine?" Jon was losing patience.

"Oh! Those were in my suitcase. The checked luggage. I didn't know if they would take them away at the airport and I've heard they don't take them out of the checked luggage. I only get a few kinds of problem-solvers from the doctor."

"Any painkillers?"

"Oh my, yes. I get very cranky without my oxy." Miss Virginia beamed. "Perhaps I should get one right now. I'm feeling a bit off and it is getting close to that time." She got up and headed for one of the bedrooms.

When she hadn't returned in five minutes, Jon got twitchy.

"Why don't you check on her?" he said to Lucille.

"Jon," Lucille murmured. "I've done enough interrogations in my day to know when you've got all you're going to get. Let her take a rest. That's the end of her story. You need to do the footwork and interview the neighbors."

Lucille was right. Virginia had finished for the evening. I was letting my mind wander, thinking about senior citizens who use taxis. A lot of them were on painkillers.

"I'll talk to her before she leaves tomorrow. Did she get a new flight?" Jon asked.

"Tomorrow afternoon. I'm picking her up at two o'clock," I confirmed.

"I'll stop by around noon," said Jon. He rose and extended his hand to me. "Join me for the game?" he asked.

Lucille smiled a woman-to-woman smile at me. Jon and I walked next door. We got through the whole first quarter.

Chapter Seven

The next morning Jon dropped me off at the garage. I checked in with Mona.

"What have you got for me?"

"Lucille to the senior center. Bridge game. She needs to be back by noon, and you and Belle are taking Virginia Percy to the airport at two."

I hooked the keys off the board and headed back to where I knew I could get coffee and a healthy breakfast. That would involve oatmeal, which would involve a chocolate chip walnut oatmeal cookie. That would mean I had oatmeal for breakfast. You can't get any healthier.

When I got to Lucille's house, I sat at the kitchen table. Miss Virginia was still sleeping in. The previous day had tired her out.

"Lucille?" I watched her take out another batch of cookies.

"Yes, dear?"

"Do you take pain killers?"

"Ah, not at the moment. I have been very lucky."

I thought about that. "Do you know Meri Edmenson?"

"Why, yes. A lovely woman. Perhaps a bit overly attached to her pet. She has an elderly cat that she dotes on. Why do you ask?"

"I take her to the senior center, so I thought maybe you had met."

94

"She doesn't play bridge. I join her for coffee occasionally. But you didn't answer my question."

"I'm just thinking about seniors and prescription meds. Herman's meds didn't help him. Meri lost hers and worries that she's losing her mind too. A lot of stuff is out of whack and meds are what they all have in common."

"We all grow old and memory is a hard thing to keep active. So, if you're done with your breakfast, I shall go see if I can sort out the dummies in my bridge game."

Lucille had finished her purse-packing routine before I arrived. We loaded into the taxi. She sat in the front seat which she said made her feel more in control. I hoped that didn't mean grabbing the steering wheel. I wasn't sure if her shadowing my foot movement was fear or anticipation. If the car responded to her, we would go a lot faster and brake a lot harder. She learned to drive on a standard transmission so her left foot hit the floor hard sometimes while her right hand twitched.

I cut through the center of town and stopped at a crosswalk. Pedestrian traffic cleared, and I crept forward. I was about to accelerate when somebody barreled in front of the cab. He cut around and snatched open the back door.

"Get me out of here," he whispered and ducked down behind the seat. It was Terry, the kid from the hospital.

I was about to tell him to get out of my cab when I saw the suit from the train station. His eyes connected with mine and he started toward us. Miraculously, traffic cleared just as he reached the crosswalk. We rocketed forward, missed the turn to the senior center and zipped up the hill. I took a quick right off Main Street and another left. By then I was well out of sight of the gorilla.

Lucille turned in her seat. "And who might you be?" she asked the young man pleasantly.

"Lucille, meet Terry. He has some drug problems and maybe some other stuff."

"Well." Lucille smiled. "Would his other problems be that big, well-dressed guy who actually seemed to be looking more at you?"

"Probably. Hey, Terry, what's happening with your oversized goon friend?"

"I think he wants to kill me." He was still scrunched down behind the seat, trying hard to be invisible.

I smiled at Lucille. "Probably just teenage drama. Maybe he wants to discuss your drug problem."

"My only drug problem is that I don't have any. At least I don't have what he wants me to have. Which would be enough of that oxy stuff he gave me to make all the teenagers in this shitty little town happy for weeks. Which is what he's looking to do."

"Nice to have a goal." I glanced over at Lucille. She was beginning to frown. "Just not that one," I said quickly.

"Perhaps we should all go to my house for a nice cup of tea and some cookies. That's what makes me feel safe," said Lucille.

What Lucille really meant was that she had a small arsenal at her house and it wasn't cookies. Her Glock would stop anyone who came uninvited to the

96

door and I was pretty sure she had some long-range weaponry as well.

I didn't know what else to do. I turned the cab in the direction of cookies and tea. Shoving Terry back onto the street didn't seem like a good idea.

"I'll call Mona and make sure I don't have any runs before we take Miss Virginia to the airport."

"I think I'll just cancel my bridge date as well." Lucille beamed and pulled her smart phone out of the baggage on her lap.

Terry sat up and watched where we were going.

I pulled up in front of Lucille's house and followed her inside. Terry cracked the car door. He looked around, scrambled out and ran in behind us.

"Where are we?" he asked, hunching over to make his tall, gawky teenage frame smaller.

"Why don't we all go in and have some refreshment before you take Ginny to the airport?" Lucille replied. Her standard answer for stress was ignoring questions and serving cookies.

We closed and bolted the door, checked the window locks, lowered shades and sat down at the table. Lucille put a plate of cookies in front of us and plugged in the teakettle.

My phone rang. "Hi, Mona."

"Where the hell are you and what the fuck is going on?"

"Lucille's and cookies. She cancelled the bridge game."

"And?" Mona was silent on the other end of the phone.

"What's happening at the garage?" I asked.

She sounded pissy already, so I didn't mention the Terry situation.

"A big goon in a suit came looking for the dumb broad with the taxi. Why did I think of you?"

"He could have meant Belle."

"He would have used the N word."

She was right. This guy wasn't one for polite conversation.

"What did you do?"

"I opened my desk drawer."

"Oh," I said. Mona was referring to the gun she kept in her desk. Whenever a dispute with a customer got as far as the garage, she opened the drawer. No one had ever challenged her.

"I'll call you before I leave with Miss Virginia."

"You'll have to tell me sooner or later who that guy was," said Mona.

"And I'll come get Belle." I turned to watch Lucille and Terry.

"She's coming to you. She'll drive," said Mona and the phone clicked off.

"Sit." Lucille commanded.

Terry sat.

"Perhaps it's time we got to know each other." She sat, rested her elbows on the table and gave Terry her "don't mess with me" stare.

"What you want to know?" Terry eyed the cookies then took an oatmeal raisin.

"How old are you?"

"As old as I need to be." There was teenage defiance and a small amount of scorn in his voice.

"Young man, I have interrogated the best liars in the known universe. So don't fuck with me." She pushed the plate of cookies across the table. Terry looked at them and looked at his empty hand.

"Have another cookie and tell me how old you are." She gave him an angelic Debbie Reynolds smile.

Terry looked over at me, maybe wondering if he should have taken his chances with the gorilla. "Fourteen, I think, maybe fifteen," he mumbled.

"Where do you live?"

"Street."

"Specificity will be appreciated."

Terry shot me a *What have you got me into?* look. "On the street, wherever. In whatever city I'm in. I know how to take care of myself."

"How do you earn a living?"

"Earn a living? I don't need to earn anything. People give me things."

"Like what things? How do you eat?" Lucille asked.

"Like I said, people give me stuff. I do something, and they give me dinner or breakfast or whatever I ask for. Sometimes money."

"What kind of things do you do for these people?"

"Jesus. I'm a street treat. Okay?" Terry's voice rose, agitated.

"Okay. Now we're getting somewhere." Lucille made tea and brought it to the table. "Tell me about the man who was in pursuit of you today. Was he a client?"

"No. Well, sort of."

"What did he want?"

"I took some of his stuff. He wanted it back and I didn't have it."

"Drugs?"

"Yeah. I was supposed to sell it to some kids downtown. I sort of lost it."

"Lost it?"

"They took it away from me. There were eight of them and one of me. The suit wanted to know who they were. He was gonna get it back."

"And you gave him their names?"

"No! God, no. I couldn't. He woulda killed them. I mean, he really would have killed at least one of them. He wanted to make an example."

"And you wouldn't give them up even though they beat you to get the drugs?"

"Hey, they were bullies, but they weren't any older than me. I know about dead. I've had some friends." Terry stopped. He looked at Lucille. He looked at me. "This isn't fair. I can't tell you this shit. I need to go."

"Where?" Lucille laid a hand over Terry's. "Terry, you're safe here as long as you want to be here. I'm not going to turn you over to child services. I won't give you up to the suit. But I need to know what's going on here. A lot of children could get hurt."

"Give me up? Give me up to the suit? You're an old lady! What can you do when that guy comes after me? Cookie him to death?"

Lucille calmly got up and went to the kitchen junk drawer.

Uh, oh, I thought and took another bite of chocolate chip.

Chapter Eight

Lucille opened the drawer, pulled out the Glock and silencer. She loaded a clip and went to the window.

"Terry?" She looked over at his astonished face. "Come here."

Terry looked at me. He rose and edged closer to Lucille.

"That red leaf out there? The one that's turning early. The color is going to be lovely this fall."

"What about the leaf?"

I took another bite of cookie and waited.

Lucille raised the Glock and fired. The leaf drifted to the ground. The bullet thumped into the tree trunk.

"Shit!" Terry backed up and stumbled over to the table. "What kind of old lady are you?"

"One who can handle that oversized, hairy thug in a suit. Clothes don't always make a man." Lucille popped out the ammo clip, removed the silencer and returned it all to the drawer. "Reminder to self. Clean gun later today." She joined us at the table, picked up her tea and took a sip.

Terry stared out the window. I admired Lucille's technique. She mixed fear, guilt and the lure of safety to reel Terry into her camp. I wondered what she would tell Jon if Terry decided to stay. I did know that Lucille was as good a liar as the ones she claimed to

101

have interrogated. I wasn't sure how well Jon could read her.

We were waiting for Terry's next move when Miss Virginia appeared in the bedroom doorway.

"Do I smell cookies? I heard a bullet to wood thump." Miss Virginia gestured in the direction of the tree without a red leaf. "My dear, you've been using the silencer again." She turned to Terry and me. "That sound is very special." She smiled.

I stared at Miss Virginia. Apparently, I wasn't the only one Lucille took out to the shooting range. Besides her dates.

Virginia turned to Terry with the infamous angel smile. Maybe she and Lucille practiced it while they were shooting big guns into man-shaped targets. "And who would this lovely young man be?" She opened her eyes wide and blinked.

Terry slouched and stared at the floor.

"Young man, when a woman enters the room, you stand up! You offer her a chair and you help her with her seat." Lucille took a step toward Terry. I thought she might cuff him on the back of his head.

Terry took one look at her face and leapt to his feet.

"Oh, no, don't stand." Miss Virginia motioned him down. I remember this game that my grandmother used to play. Young men were expected to stand and elderly women were expected to tell them to sit down. "But do tell me who you are."

"This is where you shake hands and say 'Terry, ma'am.'" Lucille was ready to take on Terry's manners as well as his evil stalker. I wondered if he had seen My Fair Lady.

Terry tentatively extended his right hand, keeping his head down, eyes focused on the table.

"Terry, what a lovely name. Now, look me in the eye and say it out loud and proud."

Terry looked up but didn't say a word. He looked over at me.

"Hey, it's easier to do what they tell you. Either one of them is a force of nature. Together, don't even ask." I shrugged my shoulders.

"My name's Terry." He touched her hand, pulled his back and sat down with a thud, trying to look smaller than his almost six-foot frame would allow.

"And where did Lucille find you?" Virginia asked.

"The taxi." This time, he looked to Lucille for guidance.

"You're doing fine. Tell her more about yourself. Where you were before you moved to Northampton, why you came here instead of, say, the moon. Why you have a large man in a suit following you and when we may expect him to arrive here." Lucille and Virginia stood close together and fixed their gazes on Terry.

"I'm not very nice."

"Oh, nonsense! You're too young to be fully formed yet. Being nice or not nice is a state of mind that only arrives with age. Like corn whiskey and fine wine." Miss Virginia smiled.

"And good sex," added Lucille. "I find men to be slow learners but once you get the basic ideas imprinted on their brains, they never forget. One needs to provide a map."

"Someone should invent a GPS for the female orgasm." Virginia sighed. The shyness she had in public disappeared when she was among female friends.

Terry turned a light shade of red. I guess he didn't rate the same kind of discretion that Miss V used around grown men like Jon.

"And speaking of *not nice*, I gather you have a stalker. Tell me more about him." Virginia paused. She seemed genuinely interested in Terry's story. "Unless you want me to ask Honey to fill me in. I gather she has had some experience with him."

"He's just some guy I met in the train station."

"How did you come to be on the train?"

"I got on in New York."

"Someone had to pay for a ticket."

"Yeah, he gave me a ticket and a prepaid charge card."

"What did he expect in return?"

"I was recruited, okay?" There was defiance in the young voice. The defiance would have been more convincing if his voice hadn't cracked to soprano. "He told me to go to Springfield on the train and there would be a cab from this company waiting for me."

"Recruited to do what?"

"I didn't ask. I just wanted to get out of where I was."

"You have no idea what he wanted from you."

"I do now." This time he pushed the teenage attitude.

Lucille and Virginia waited.

Nothing further came from Terry.

"And what would that be?" Lucille prodded.

"He's dealing scrips," Terry mumbled. "He needed someone younger to deal to the local school kids. He stood out like a big turd on the sidewalk."

"Prescription drugs," said Lucille. "He wanted you to be his turd. Have another cookie." She shoved the plate closer to Terry.

Terry slumped farther down in his chair.

A car pulled into the shared driveway between Lucille's side of the house and Jon's side. It could be Jon, or it could be Belle arriving to help deliver Virginia to the airport. I went to the window and peeked out. It was Belle, thank God. Terry and Lucille would have to work out an arrangement without me.

We loaded Virginia and her luggage into the car. Belle took the wheel and I rode shotgun. Miss V preferred to avoid the temptation to grab the steering-wheel, an impulse she found overwhelming when she rode in front.

We wove through town, dodging pedestrians, potholes and parking trollers, finally reaching the on ramp to the interstate. Traffic was heavy, but I noticed an SUV close to our rear end for the last few blocks.

"We have a tailgater." Belle tapped the brakes a few times to tell him to back off. He didn't.

She merged onto the highway, figuring he would use the passing lane. He didn't.

"Back off, asshole," she muttered.

I turned around to see a huge black SUV. It swerved into the passing lane and I noticed the fancy chrome wheels and sunroof. I knew it had a sunroof because a head popped up through it. Trying to pretend one is a politician or the Pope at fifteen or twenty mph is okay, but at sixty-five it doesn't play as well. He ducked down again.

"Hey, I know that guy! It's the bubba Lucille shot in the foot in the flower and gun shop. Why is he following us? We didn't shoot him."

I watched the SUV. The body popped up again. The gun he was holding wavered in the wind and then jumped a few times.

"I think he might be shooting at us."

"What!?" Belle pushed her foot down and our little car leapt forward.

An ancient farm truck with manure and chicken feathers piled above its side panels lumbered ahead of us. We had our windows rolled up but the rancid odor still crept in. I couldn't imagine how the nose popping out of the sunroof was dealing with it. We came up on the manure truck fast but the SUV was still a dark shadow right behind us.

The top-heavy load of chicken poop jiggled and swayed. A stray feather drifted onto our windshield.

"Watch out for that truck. The load doesn't look very stable." I held onto the sissy hold.

"Uh hunh," murmured Belle. "Bullets make me unstable. Hold on!" she yelled.

Swinging to the left lane, she scraped our small car by the truck and swerved back, barely missing the front fender. A horn blasted and brakes screeched as the SUV pulled next to the truck. But the truck tilted, its load swaying precariously. I looked away as Belle nailed the "go" pedal.

"Mr. SUV still behind us?"

I was still gripping the sissy hold and Miss Virginia was lying flat down sideways in the back seat.

106

I craned my head around to look. "Nope."

Chapter Nine

Belle slowed to a sedate 70 mph and we continued to the airport.

Miss V sat up, smiling. She took the whole incident with remarkable calm.

When we pulled up to the terminal, I trotted inside and grabbed a wheelchair. We loaded up Miss Virginia and I pushed her to security.

Belle went off to hang with the limo drivers.

Miss V and I lined up with all the other senior citizens to one side of the x-ray pass through. Everyone began comparing notes on hip, ankle or knee replacements. All that metal meant that security had to pass the hand wand over each one of the elders.

I figured the combined years of life experience in that line could solve all the problems of civilization if we would only listen. On the other hand, sometimes they were difficult to understand. Each complaint, statement or question was greeted with a chorus of "WHAT?"

Twenty minutes later, I called Belle, and she swooped in to pick me up. Miss V and her titanium knee were on the way to Savannah.

"So, what was he after?" Belle asked as she merged onto the interstate.

"The guy in the SUV? I have no idea. Maybe he thought Miss V was Lucille. Revenge?"

"Where would he get a car like that? Last time you saw him he was holding up a gun store because he couldn't afford to buy flowers. And he was on foot."

"Someone else was driving this time. Maybe it was the driver's car."

"Someone hiring local talent to shoot taxi drivers and old ladies? Thugs are us?"

"I got no idea."

By the time we got back to town we had exhausted all possibilities about why the bubba was following us, shooting at us and why us. We didn't have any good answers so we let it go.

"I hope the fuckers eat that shit," said Belle as she steered off the interstate and turned right toward town. There was a tow truck pulled over at the end of the off ramp with an SUV hanging from the hook. The suspended vehicle was too covered with chicken shit inside and out to tell what color it was. It did have really fancy chrome wheels, though.

"Hunh," said Belle and drove us back to the Cool Rides garage.

I went in to see if Mona had any fast fares that might help fund a new pair of boots for my fall wardrobe and maybe pay the rent.

"Got a delivery to Springfield. Ezekiel Grumowski wants us to pick up his Viagra in Northampton and deliver it. He says to hurry. He has an appointment tonight and he needs to be ready. Usually Willie takes this one, but he's in Boston."

Belle came in behind me. "So, how old is this guy he needs Viagra, and who's the appointment with? I might know her. Sometimes it's nice to see some of my friends from before."

"All I know is he uses a pharmacy here because he doesn't like the guy down in Springfield. He's ninety-three and I have no idea who he uses when the Viagra kicks in. Do I look like a pimp?"

"No, you really, really don't. But with a little time, I could help you with that. The shoes alone would be worth the effort. And we would call you a *madam* in the business."

I snatched the fare slip out of Mona's hand.

"Take the stealth car and both of you need to go," she said and slammed the door to her office.

Willie didn't want his drivers going into the Springfield neighborhoods alone, so we traveled in pairs. He had a special taxi that he had disguised as a beater car that no one would want to steal or even swipe the CD player, radio, or even fuzzy dice hanging from the rear-view because it didn't have any of those luxuries. There was a portable GPS unit that we took with us when we left the car. It had livery plates, but we usually mudded out the livery label. It was an aging white Toyota Corolla. There were so many beater Toyotas on the road that no one ever remembered seeing it. Besides being good to go into sketchy neighborhoods, it would be the ultimate hold up vehicle. Just in case we wanted to add to my boot fund.

Mona leaned out of her office. "It's prepaid by his trust fund but he usually tips in cash. And remember to mud out the livery."

"Right, a ninety-three-year-old with a trust fund," I mumbled, wishing I had a trust fund that would last to ninety-three or even until tomorrow. By the time I got out to the car, Belle had finished smearing the livery off the license plate and was waiting behind the

110

wheel. Willie had added another dent to the driver's side door, deep enough to show but not enough to disturb the function of the door or break the paint. There was a scratch along the back side and a rust spot on the fender. The wheels looked like they came from the side of the road.

I rode shotgun and we motored off to the pharmacy. We never asked Willie what he had put under the hood, but it took off like a fighter jet. We took the corner fast enough to know he had added something to the suspension as well.

We pulled into parking for the grocery/liquor/deli/ pharmacy store and I trotted inside. Since the prescription had been called in and the pharmacist knew Cool Rides would pick it up, I figured it would be fast. But I was a new face and the car was not the usual one so he needed to see my identification and then call Mona to make sure.

Belle had no patience and she walked in behind me just as the pharmacist came out from behind his medicine counter. He handed me a white bag.

I was about to sign for it when a guy in a hoodie and baggy pants pushed Belle out of the way and butted in front of me.

"I want all your oxy stuff," he screamed.

I stepped back a few feet. The hoodie pulled a gun out of the back of his pants, which threatened to slip down to his knees but somehow didn't. His hand was shaking like a dead leaf about to fall and I hoped he didn't pull the trigger by accident.

Belle grunted, slid her oversized bag off her shoulder and swung it in a long arc. She connected with the side of hoodie's head and he went down on his knees. She let the bag swing back the other direction and he face-planted on the floor. His gun flew out and shot the potted plant that was between the pharmacy and the grocery store.

"Holy shit!" said the pharmacist.

"I got the cops on speed dial. They're on the way," said the clerk who was peering over the storage area.

"Hunh, maybe we should leave now." Belle started to the door. "We need to get that scrip to Ezekiel in time."

"Maybe you want to get your duct tape out before he wakes up," I said to the clerk. I used the pharmacy pen to pick up the gun then slid it off onto the counter. "Call us if you need us," I said as I jogged out the door.

I joined Belle in the car. We whizzed off toward the interstate. The first police car pulled into the parking lot as we were heading down the street. I saw Jon's unmarked pull in behind it but since we were in the car with the cloak of invisibility, he didn't notice us. The pharmacist would squeal on us so Jon would find out but I could face that problem later.

Twenty minutes later we were winding through the tougher neighborhoods of Springfield. Our GPS softly informed us that our destination was 100 feet ahead on the right. There was a note of desperation in her voice when she told us "You have reached your destination."

Belle removed the portable GPS and stashed it in her bag. We parked in front and walked up the steps to a dilapidated house tucked between two three-story tenements.

I was about to knock on the door, hoping it wouldn't cave in with the pressure, when a black

Cadillac Escalade screeched around the corner. Next door the ground floor window flew open and an Uzi submachine gun poked out. We ducked behind the concrete steps as the big gun let loose. A rocket launcher came out of the Escalade's window. We heard an ear-splitting bang and the tree above our invisible car exploded. A branch broke off, squashed the trunk and rolled off onto the pavement. The Escalade took off, sideswiping our car and removing the side-view mirror.

Ezekiel's door flew open. "Goddamn drug dealers! I got a meth lab on one side and an oxy ring on the other. Shit for neighbors," he muttered. "You bring my stuff? Get in here. Hope he remembered the pain killers. I usually pop an oxy after. Sometimes another the next morning. My joints aren't always as up as other parts of me."

We scrambled inside. Ezekiel looked every day of his ninety-three years. He was bent at the waist and his pants rode high over his pot belly. He was the opposite of the gang banger from the pharmacy. I wondered how the gang banger would look at ninety-three. That is, if he made it past thirty.

"What? You never seen an old man with a hard on? Us old geezers like an orgasm as much as you young chickies. In this neighborhood, I can't go out looking for it. I gotta have it come to me. Goddamn kids. Hey, I know you," he said, looking at Belle. "You ever provide services?"

"Not to you honey, but I brought a friend here once. She introduced us. Chaz? You remember her? A specialty kind of ho."

"Oh, yeah, really good with her tongue. Never forget that one." Ezekiel took his meds from me and handed us each a ten-dollar bill. He opened the bag and peered inside. "Yup, there's a few pain killers in here too. I'll use 'em tomorrow."

Belle opened the door cautiously. No big black SUV, no rocket launchers.

I jumped when Ezekiel patted me on the ass. "Hope it's you next time. Better on the eyes than Willie." He grinned.

I swatted his hand away and slid outside. "When did ninety become the new thirty?" I asked Belle.

We contemplated the stealth car for a few minutes.

"Its cloak of invisibility just got another layer put on. Maybe we should've put some of Ezekiel's drugs in the gas tank," Belle said.

"We all need something to pop our clutches," I sighed.

"Let's see if it goes. Like before we call Mona."

We got in. It started. I gently pushed down on the accelerator. The car crept forward. No major thumps, no flat tires, no important parts broken. But no one would put anything in the trunk for a while.

We got back to Cool Rides without mishap. Mona didn't have anything for us and it was end of shift so I took the taxi and drove to Jon's house. I stood in front of the two doors. Jon was still at work. At least Lucille would be more entertaining than an empty house. And she might still have Terry with her. I knocked on her door.

Terry opened it.

Lucille was standing in the kitchen, inching open her junk drawer. She moved away and over to the cookie platter when she saw me.

"Always check from the window first. I must get Jon to put in a peep hole." She scolded Terry and started stacking more cookies on the plate. "Terry and I have been surfing." Lucille patted her computer, affectionately known as Baby. "It turns out that my great nephew is quite computer literate. He helped me find the best Viagra ad I've seen yet. Featuring a full-blown stiffy."

Terry slouched down, stuffed a cookie into his mouth and grabbed the glass of milk.

"Your great nephew?" I looked at Terry's skinny self. He wouldn't be skinny for long if he stayed in Lucille's house. He might also learn a few new tricks about how to lie with conviction.

"Terry has agreed to stay here while my sister's daughter is recuperating from a slight accident."

"What happened to the sister I never knew you had?"

"She entered a combat bridge tournament. Her daughter, Terry's mother, came to her defense." Lucille sighed. "My sister needed a hip replacement and her daughter had some quick facial reconstruction. She just couldn't take care of a teenager at the same time. I have been entrusted with his wellbeing."

I groaned. One of the best liars in the known universe. "So, you guys are spending time surfing porn sites?"

"Certainly not. We're looking at possible sources of the oxy drugs."

Terry looked up with surprise on his face. "We are?"

"Of course. I always say, follow the money. If you can't do that, follow the drugs." Lucille smiled.

While I was busy pushing Miss Virginia past the zealous protectors of air travelers, Lucille had put her interrogation techniques to use on Terry. His teenage defiance and snotty attitude shriveled. When he was done talking, Lucille had a good idea of who the suit was and what he was doing in small town New England. Terry had known more than he realized about the local dealings of the prescription drug trade. He might also have decided that he was better off with Lucille and her cookies, big guns and fixation on dildos than he would be out on the street playing dodge 'em with that gorilla in a suit.

"Terry listens better than many teenagers. He has some provocative information."

"So, we should call Jon?" I was ready to pass this one onto someone with more weaponry than I had. That would have been anyone.

"Oh, I don't think we're ready to call in the law," said Lucille.

Terry fidgeted and slouched lower.

"What we have is mostly conjecture and seen through the eyes of a frightened teenaged boy."

"Hey, I'm not scared and I'm not a boy. I just heard enough to know what this guy wants to do."

"Yes, and I think we should begin by gathering hard evidence."

"Just what is it that he wants to do?" I turned to Terry.

"Deal nasty drugs to innocent children," Lucille said self-righteously.

"Or some not so innocent," Terry mumbled.

"Apparently he has good sources for the drugs coming up from the south, but he lacks a local distribution network. There also seems to be some competition in this area that he is trying to eliminate. Mostly local drugs being bought and sold to more southern markets. Do you understand all this?" Lucille addressed both Terry and me.

"I understand that the police can gather evidence better than I can. Maybe even better than you." I addressed this to Lucille.

"Nonsense. I'm far more believable undercover in this operation than Jon could ever be."

"But you are going to tell him, right?" I knew from Lucille's expression that it was unlikely. My big question was how much of this I could or wanted to keep from Jon.

"I'm thinking of moving to Virginia's house until she returns."

"What? Why? She's gone for two weeks. How is that going to help you?"

"Living next door to the law will impede my investigation. I would like to go over there immediately."

"Immediately as in tonight?" I gulped.

"Now," said Lucille.

Lucille was a steam roller. Once she had an idea, everything in her way got flattened. Jon would disapprove of Lucille looking into the lives of people who could be dangerous or even fatal. So, she wouldn't tell him and she would expect Terry and me to keep quiet too. And then there was Terry. Jon hadn't even met him yet.

"Do you have a plan or are you just going to wing it?"

"I always have a plan. It has its own wings, so I don't need to fly, if you insist on metaphors."

"Can we discuss it?"

"It's *need to know* and I know how good Jon is at getting information out of people. And those are people he doesn't like. So, no, you don't need to know."

I kept quiet, figuring I could get more details out of Terry later. Lucille had developed a maternal attitude toward Terry and I was pretty sure she would take him with her. Thus he would probably be privy to the plan.

I watched Lucille bring out her short stay bag. She set it on the dining room table and tossed in a sexy nightgown. Her toiletries and extra underwear went on top of that and an extra light sweater, two dresses, the silencer, extra ammo and the Glock.

I looked at the gun and then at Lucille.

"Ginny had a home invasion. I intend to find out why and not get injured in the process." She looked at me indignantly. She packed up her computer in a separate carrying case.

Terry didn't have anything to pack.

Lucille wrote a note to Jon that she was taking care of Miss Virginia's plants, and we all trooped out to the taxi.

When we arrived at Miss V's house, I carried Lucille's suitcase and the computer to the doorstep.

Lucille walked over to the front window, disappeared behind a bush and returned with a key. "Ginny really did ask me to keep an eye on the house. She didn't know I would move in, but I'll email her."

We all went inside, and Lucille took her bags into one of the bedrooms.

Terry stood looking around like a lost puppy worried that it had peed on the floor again but not quite sure. He didn't seem to know how to handle someone being nice and giving orders at the same time. I resisted patting him on the head and moved back to the front door.

Lucille came out of the bedroom. "That one is where you will be sleeping. We will go shopping for some better clothing for you as well. You can't sleep in your street clothes and naked doesn't work if there is an emergency. One can't attend to a fire fight with no clothes on."

I edged toward the door, anticipating that Lucille would try to draw me into something I was sure I should not be part of.

"Honey? We will need a ride first thing tomorrow morning to find new attire for my nephew. Will you tell Mona to send someone over around ten o'clock? Perhaps it should be Belle. She won't have any conflict of interest."

"You don't think the judge is a conflict of interest?"

"She isn't involved enough with him to be a problem. Too early in the relationship. And Belle has a better poker face. She lies better than you do."

I couldn't decide whether to be insulted, hurt or complimented. I went with, "I'm leaving now. I'm going to spend tomorrow making a living."

I dropped off the taxi and walked to my apartment. I wanted to avoid seeing Jon for a night. He would know something was up within five minutes of saying hello to me. This way, I could sleep on whatever it was that I didn't want to tell him. And maybe Lucille would come to her senses by morning. Not likely but possible.

When I got to Miss Virginia's house the next morning Lucille was in the kitchen. She was opening and slamming cupboard doors. She stuck her head in the refrigerator and took it out again. Terry was sitting at the table eating a piece of toast with something strange smeared on it.

"What are you doing here?" She stared at me.

"You wanted to take Terry shopping this morning. I didn't have any other appointments until ten o'clock. I thought I could run you over to wherever."

"Terry found some clothing in Ginny's husband's closet. I guess she hasn't cleaned out his belongings since he passed. And I'll take him to the Goodwill store. He'll be going through clothes quickly as he is that age." Lucille opened another cupboard. "There is simply nothing here that can be used in a decent cookie batter." She had peanut butter, canned ham, tomato soup, and tuna fish sitting on the counter.

I decided to leave Lucille to her scary cookie makings. I had my hand on the door handle when the land line rang.

Lucille stomped over and jerked off its cradle. "Miss Virginia's residence."

The voice on the other end was talking loudly as if he might be hard of hearing.

"Miss V? Is this Miss V? I need Miss V," the voice echoed into the room.

"I'm sorry but she isn't here at the moment. Perhaps I can take a message or help you somehow." Lucille picked up that the person was hard of hearing and raised her voice.

"She said to call her when I wanted money bad enough. Well, I need something to eat and I ain't got nothing left but some of these stupid pills. She want 'em or what?"

"My dear, I have no idea. But I will tell you that there is a free lunch today at the Methodist Church. Will that be helpful?"

"How am I gonna git there? I can barely git out my door."

"I'll send someone over for you. Be ready at twelve o'clock and don't be late. Where should she pick you up?"

"Who the hell is this? And where is Miss V?"

"I'm taking care of things for her while she's away."

The phone clicked. Lucille held it away from her ear, studying it. "What a strange call," she said and picked up a can of soup. "I wonder how this would taste with chocolate chips. I don't think so." She laid it back on the counter.

I slipped out and drove to the Cool Rides garage.

Mona came out of the office as I drove up.

"I need you to run dispatch for the next two hours." She handed me a cell phone and gestured toward the land line. "That too."

Mona walked out the door and got in the cab I had just left. She hadn't closed the door before the cell phone rang. She slammed the door shut and kicked up gravel leaving the parking lot.

"Cool Rides, where are you and where would you like to be?"

"I need a ride to church. How much is it gonna cost?"

"Where are you?"

"Park Avenue."

"And the church?"

"3rd Street."

"Sir, what city are you in?"

"Huh?"

"Where are you?"

"Park Avenue."

"In what city?"

"What city? Is there more than one city? New York! Where'd you think I was? Where are you?"

"I'm in Massachusetts. Where did you get our number?"

"The Internet. You shouldn't say you are where you aren't."

"Sir..." I heard a click and the cell phone went dead.

Sometimes I love the Internet, sometimes I hate it. I sat in Mona's chair and started playing solitaire on her computer. The land line rang.

"Hey, I need a ride fast. How soon can you get here?"

"Where is here?"

"The bank branch in the Walmart plaza. But I need it like right now."

"I can get a car to you in ten minutes."

"Shit, that's too late."

I heard sirens in the background. They got louder.

"Fuck, it's the cops. Never mind." The phone went dead.

I leaned back in Mona's chair and hit the TV remote. The local news was on. I watched the cops collar the robber fifty feet from the bank. The picture bounced as the cameraman ran to catch up. The cop jerked the phone out of the would-be robber's hand.

The land line rang.

When the cop who hit redial stopped laughing, I flipped the TV off. It wasn't as entertaining as watching O.J. lead the parade but it helped pass the time. Dispatch can be crazy busy. It can also be boring, boring, boring.

Belle called in. She finished running a bald biker guy with a Harley tattoo to the yarn store to get a pattern for a baby blanket. "Anything new for me? I think I'll stop for coffee."

"Keep your phone next to your ear."

"Roger that." She clicked off.

Five minutes later I called Belle. "You got a guy says he was abducted by aliens out on route five and ten next to the Irish Inn. He wants a ride back to town."

"You get his cell phone?"

"Nope, he wouldn't give it out because the aliens might be listening in. And he sounded in a hurry."

"Okey dokey."

She called back in ten minutes. "I see the guy. He hasn't got any clothes."

"Like naked?"

"Except for his cell phone. That doesn't worry me. I can handle some skin. But no clothes means no wallet."

"Yeah?"

"Where's the fare money?"

"Yeah, that might be a problem."

"Wait, he's waving money at me. I don't want to know where he hid it."

"Go get him."

"I'm leaving the phone on speaker. Just in case the aliens are listening."

I heard the cab door open.

"I need tinfoil. You got tinfoil? Can we stop and buy some?"

Belle answered, "There's a wait fee. And pants might be more important than tinfoil."

Belle arrived back at the garage wearing a platter shaped tinfoil hat. "Just in case." She grinned. "He had a wad of twenties. We stopped and bought five boxes of tinfoil. Well, I got the tinfoil. I didn't think he should go into the store with his junk hanging. So, I helped him make a hat and jock strap out of tinfoil. He paid me a fashion consultant fee." She handed me fifty dollars and a carton of tinfoil. "I dropped him at the courthouse."

"The courthouse? Is that where his spaceship is landing."

"Nope. But he's angling for an insanity defense."

"What did he do?"

"Mugged a Girl Scout for her Thin Mints. Too bad for him she'd just finished her merit badge in karate and knot tying. She put him down and trussed him like a rodeo calf with her little yellow scarf," said Belle, smiling wider.

I sent Belle to drop Lucille at the senior center and Terry at Goodwill. Apparently Miss Virginia's husband did not have the same fashion sense as your average teenager. Terry argued that he didn't want to stick out like a mafia goon in a schoolyard. Lucille had to agree with that.

"Lucille keeps getting phone calls about Miss V handing out cash to seniors. What's that about?" she asked when she got back.

"I got no idea. How are her cookies?"

"Not. Tomato soup doesn't work as a cookie ingredient." Belle paused. "You going to Jon's tonight?"

I thought about Jon's big screen TV and other things. "Yeah, probably. Why?"

"Just asking. I'm going to dinner with the Judge."

"Yeah? What are you wearing?"

"The best shoes money can buy."

"What shoes?" asked Mona, walking through the door as the phone rang.

Riggs pulled into the parking lot and Willie came in from the garage area. The phone calls were all "how much?" calls, so Belle and Riggs went outside.

They sat in the wobbly plastic chairs, taking a break and playing their latest fashion terrorist game.

"Hey, look at that one." Belle giggled as a middle-aged woman wearing the relaxed linen look strode by on the other side of the street.

"Who's her designer, Rip Van Wrinkle? Looks like she slept in that shirt for twenty years." Riggs high-fived Belle and they both laughed out loud.

125

A teenager with the waist-at-the-knees pant style sauntered down the sidewalk.

"Wooo, wooo!" Belle pumped her fist. "How do you avoid pursuit in those? Don't try a hold up in that outfit."

Riggs waved in the direction of a maybe teenager. "Talk about ass flossing. She's combined it with the ever-stylish muffin top fat roll. Ooh! And dig the tramp stamp on the backside of the muffin."

"You know what they say about muffin tops? No one wants the bottoms." Belle and Riggs did a low five.

The comments were getting snarky.

They kept up a continuous stream of put downs until a black SUV drove up close to the parking area.

"Ooh, evil-looking," said Belle. She squinted at the oversized vehicle. "Hey, I've seen that humungo elephant before."

There was a pop and another louder pop, then a big bang and one of the tires on the car Belle had just parked deflated. Two more loud bangs, two more tires sank to the gravel.

"What the hell?" Belle leapt to her feet. The SUV sped off with a squeal of tires.

Willie came charging out of the office, shaking his fist. He stood in the middle of the street and whipped out his cell phone.

"Get over here fast. We just had a drive by." Willie had Jon on speed dial.

Chapter Ten

"No, no one was hurt except the cars. Four brand-fucking new tires shot out." Willie paced around the parking lot examining the cars for dents and scratches.

Five minutes later Jon arrived with the forensics van in tow. The forensic team swarmed over and under the cars, their gloved hands snatching up bullets and depositing them in bags.

One of the techs came over to Jon who was standing next to Willie.

"Most of them passed through the tires but..." He looked at the tires. "Since you have to take the tires off anyway, maybe we could do it now and recover the rest. We found some casing by the sidewalk." He pointed to where the SUV had stopped to take aim.

"Do whatever you need to catch the bastards," said Willie. He stormed off into the garage area to grieve for the tires.

I wanted to mention that none of the humans got holes and deflated but he already knew that.

Jon came over to where Belle, Riggs and I were huddled, standing with the cars between us and anyone who might make another swing by. "I need to talk to all of you and get a clear picture of what happened. Belle, you ready to sit down? We can use Mona's office."

127

"Damn tootin'. That's the second time those idiots have shot guns off around me. Third time for Honey."

Jon raised his eyebrows and stared at me. "We'll talk as soon as I get Belle's statement." He and Belle walked into the office and Jon closed the door. I watched Belle move around the tiny space. I understood why she couldn't sit still. I was having trouble myself but watching the tech team kept my brain from going into overdrive.

Half an hour later Belle and Jon came out. Jon held the door and motioned me in.

When I sat in the visitor's chair he leaned his butt on the edge of the desk.

"Tell me your version of what just happened."

I'd barely had time to notice anything before the SUV was gone. All I could say was that I had seen a black SUV and heard the gunshots.

"Had you seen any of the people in the SUV before?"

"I didn't see them this time. By the time I realized they were there, they were gone."

"Had you seen the car before?"

"Maybe, but except for my taxi, I'm not a car person. All those big black cars look the same to me."

"Tell me about the incident on the highway going to the airport."

"Oh." I looked down at my hands, stalling. I didn't know how much Belle had told him. "A black SUV tailgated us and then shot out of their sunroof at us. I guess they had a little accident that made them stop."

"What type of accident?"

"One involving chicken manure."

My version must have been the same as Belle's. Jon moved on to the hold up in Guns and Daisies. I had made the mistake of telling Belle about it.

"The guy on the highway might have been the same guy. Only he seemed to have had an equipment upgrade. He had a gun and a car and a driver."

"Lucille was with you in the store and Miss Virginia was in the car going to the airport? And you didn't report either incident?"

"No one got hurt." I wasn't about to tell Jon how much the taxi companies in his safe little town didn't share with the cops. We frequently dealt with people who habitually broke the law. If we stopped to fill out a report every time we saw something illegal, we would never get to drive.

Jon sighed. "And speaking of Lucille, have you seen her recently?"

"She's taking care of Miss Virginia's plants. She moved over there temporarily."

"Okay. Have you seen the kid you left at the hospital?"

I guessed the uniform who interviewed me reported the event to Jon. I asked anyway, "How'd you know about that?"

"Some paper crossed my desk with your name on it. The hospital wants to get paid. And I'd like to talk to that kid." Jon looked unhappy about my involvement, but he didn't have time to sort it out and scream at me.

"Umm."

"Honey? Where the hell is he?" Jon stood up and leaned over me. His nose was inches from mine and his eyes were not in seduction mode.

129

I slouched down in the chair. Lucille could take care of Jon without my help. "With Lucille," I said.

"Lucille?" Jon looked blank. "At Miss Virginia's house? Why?"

I told him the short version. It included Terry jumping into my cab. It didn't include the big gorilla in a suit. I figured Lucille could add that if she wanted to. If Jon got it in his mind that I was in danger my driving would be severely curtailed. If he could concentrate on Lucille and Terry for a while it might take his focus off me.

There was a knock on the door, which was silly because it was glass. We could see Willie outside. Jon motioned him in.

"I don't know what those fuckers want from me, but they need to be stopped." Willie tried to pace in a circle but there wasn't any room. Every time he turned around, he was in my lap or Jon's face.

"Did you get a license plate?"

"It was covered."

"Did you recognize any of them?"

"They didn't stick their heads out and the windows were tinted. I was inside so my view wasn't too good."

Jon turned to me with a question in his eyes.

"I didn't see their faces, but Belle thought it was the same car that took a shot at us on the highway."

"I'm going to get those tires changed, make sure there's no damage to the cars." Willie left.

"I'm going to talk to Lucille. I'll pick you up in an hour." Jon's eyes softened slightly. "Spend the night at my house. It's safer." He took one of my hands.

"Please." Maybe he was learning. Or maybe he was getting better at manipulating me.

I was still inside Mona's office watching the fuss over the cars outside when the land line rang. I picked it up.

"Where the fuck is the kid?" A male voice growled into my ear.

"Huh?" I wasn't on the right planet for this. My mind was still thinking about the sound of gun fire way too close to my body.

"You been warned. I want that kid." The phone clicked dead.

Okay, now I knew what the gorilla guy wanted, but not why. I wasn't going to snitch on Terry, but I definitely needed to talk to Lucille. And I needed to interact somehow with Jon the cop.

Willie stared mournfully at the cars. Riggs went on a prearranged airport run in the car with four good tires. I decided to talk to Belle. She had more experience with the criminal element even though I was the only one who had actually done jail time. I walked out and handed the office phone to Mona. I didn't mention the gorilla call.

"Want to get some coffee?" I asked Belle.

"I sure as hell won't be driving for a while." She sighed morosely, looking at the cars. There was only one without any holes in its tires. The goons had managed to hit one tire on each of four cars. "Those super shoes just got a little further away. Guess the Judge will have to love me for my other attributes."

Mona looked up. "Be back in an hour or less and keep those cell phones glued to your bodies. I'll have

131

a car up and running faster than a cheetah taped to your granny's back."

Belle and I trudged uptown to the Cup and Sip. I indulged in the super diet—what came over me?—version of black coffee.

My cell phone rang as the barista handed over my grande caramel mocha extra hot with whip, chocolate sprinkles and syrup. I hit the "hi" button.

"Where is Lucille?" asked Jon.

"She's staying at Virginia's."

"I'm there and she's not."

"Maybe she went to her house to get baking supplies."

"In what? She doesn't have a car."

"Maybe a friend? Belle and I can check her house and see if she's there. We have Belle's car."

"Call me as soon as you get there."

We rounded the corner to Lucille's house. A black SUV sat by the curb. It seemed smaller than I remembered. Probably because there weren't any guns sticking out the windows. Then I realized that all four tires were flat.

Belle drove her Mini by the SUV. Even with flat tires it was too tall to see in the windows but no guns poked out as we drove by. I took that as a good sign. Belle pulled a u-turn and parked behind the SUV. We got out and approached it cautiously. I noticed a few white feathers stuck to the back bumper. It was empty. The driver's window was down. There was a smear of blood and a dent in the door.

Lucille's front door swung open.

"They left. As well they should. They clearly were not here for cookies."

I called Jon.

"She's here. She's fine. I guess a friend gave her a ride."

"Tell her to stay there. I'm tied up at the station, so I'll be a few hours."

Like I could tell Lucille to stay.

I went inside to heavenly aromas.

"Where do you think they went, the guys from that big black ugly car?" I asked.

"I imagine they went to the hospital."

I looked over at Belle and Terry who were squaring off over the last cookie. "Why would they go to the hospital?"

"To stop the bleeding." Lucille took another batch of cookies out of the oven and shoveled them onto the platter, averting the pending war.

"What was bleeding?"

Terry grinned through a mouthful of cookie. "She shot the driver's finger off. He had his hand hanging out the window with a big gun. He dropped the gun, so she walked over and shot out the tires."

"She always aims for the smallest appendage." I smiled back at Terry.

"Preemptive strike is best if you can't avoid the situation," said Lucille. "And don't exaggerate young man. It was only the tip of his pinky. My, but those kinds of wounds bleed a lot." She turned to me. "And I don't believe it was his smallest appendage. Men like that tend to need to compensate."

Belle smiled. Terry's grin widened. I grabbed a cookie.

"How did they leave?" I asked.

"Oh, another black car came and picked them up."

133

"Where's their gun?" I asked.

Lucille pointed to the junk drawer.

We were all considering what we should do next when a tow truck came around the corner. The driver backed up to the SUV and crawled under the front end. He attached the hook and stood up. He kicked the side of the SUV.

He swore creatively and screamed at the car. "I ain't gonna fix you again. You're the car from hell. Chicken shit, flat tires, blood, dents. You're cursed!" He got in the tow truck and drove off with the black SUV thumping crookedly behind.

"Probably should have brought a flat bed. That's gonna be hell on the suspension. Kind of makes up for the drive by at the garage," said Belle.

"I think he wants to make sure they don't call him again," I said, wondering who they might be.

"How did they find you?"

"They came to Virginia's house." Lucille thought for a moment. "I got the strangest phone call from one of the personal care attendants I know. He's a drifter." She looked at my blank expression and added, "He works at different locations rather than being employed by an agency. Anyway, he called Virginia's house about some money she owed him. He must have helped her on some occasion, although I never knew her to use a PCA. When I told him she was out of town he seemed upset. But he agreed to come get us and transport us here so I could get a supply of cookies made up. Virginia has absolutely nothing in her kitchen. Honestly, you never really know people, do you?"

"And the goons just followed you and hung guns out the window?" I couldn't figure out if they were focused on Lucille, Terry, or someone we didn't even know about.

"I think they were watching Virginia's house. Maybe because of the home invasion, they thought she had something worth stealing. Anyway, I was getting too many phone calls at Ginny's house. I had no idea she had such an active social life."

"What kind of phone calls?" asked Belle, who was still busy eating cookies.

"Mostly about money she owed."

"Was she living on Social Security? That can be hard. But she didn't seem to be suffering financially," I said.

"You think she would borrow more than she could pay back?" asked Belle.

"She could have come to me if she needed money. She knew that," said Lucille.

"How long have you known Virginia?" asked Belle.

Lucille stared out the window. "At least two years. I met her at the senior center over a bridge game. She found the competition pointless. But we became friends over our mutual interest in erotic literature." Belle smiled and glanced at me.

"Maybe gorilla man is a debt collector," I said, trying to keep the conversation off Lucille's taste in literature.

"There's a good-sized book club at the senior center that meets over that shared interest." Lucille stuck to the wrong subject.

I turned to Terry, figuring he would flee that discussion like a tick off a dead dog.

"Maybe you know something about that guy that you don't know you know." I told them about the phone call we'd gotten after the drive-by at the Cool Rides garage. "That guy is pretty focused on getting hold of you."

"I knew him from New York. He thought I would help him with other kids. Fit in when he couldn't."

Lucille put a protective hand on Terry's shoulder. "Terry fit into that horrid man's business plan. The bigger question is, who does that man work for? Did you get any feeling that he was the boss?"

Terry squirmed. He stared out the window for a second. "I know who he worked for in New York. And I know he likes boys." He looked away from us again. "Those guys he worked for? They don't like that."

"Ah, well, those two facts might account for his tenacity in tracking you down," said Lucille. "The big question is whether he wants to kill you or make you his boy toy."

Terry looked depressed. "I think it's the boy toy thing. He really got off on me."

Lucille patted his shoulder. "How did you feel about him?" she asked.

I swallowed wrong and started coughing. I wasn't sure Terry felt comfortable talking about his sexual preferences to three women.

"I hated what he wanted. But it gave me control. He fed me and gave me money and drugs." Terry looked at me. "You pretty much know the rest. I wasn't supposed to use the drugs myself. They were for selling to some kids up here. But I'd never tried the oxy stuff so I just swallowed a bunch."

I was going to ask Terry more about how much he took when we heard a car pull into the driveway.

Chapter Eleven

A door slammed. Five seconds later, the handle on Lucille's door turned. Of course, Lucille had installed three new locks, so nothing happened.

"Open the damn door, Lucille!" shouted Jon.

"Oh, hold your balls together." Lucille returned the greeting.

She threw the top lock, got a key on the middle lock and bolted back the bottom. Anybody wanting to get into Lucille's house could have broken a window, but they wouldn't get in the door. Jon came in and glanced around at the group. His gaze settled on Terry.

Belle pushed away from the table, ready to leave now that the law had arrived.

"You must be Honey's friend." Jon's eyes moved around the room. "And now Lucille's and Belle's as well." His mouth twitched. "You might want to be careful. These three ladies can be lethal."

"Sit down, Jon," said Lucille. "Have a cookie." She was using her *FBI, I'm-in-charge* voice. I wasn't sure it worked on Jon, but he sat and picked up a cookie. He was in blue jeans and a sweatshirt, so he was off duty. Unfortunately, that didn't make him any less of a cop. He could be very charming if the stakes were high enough and I was betting that Terry was high stakes in this particular mystery of prescription drugs and drive-by shootings.

Belle stood up, stretched and mumbled. "I gotta get to bed, early ride."

I had checked the board at Cool Rides and there were no early rides, but I didn't want to spoil her excuse for leaving since I planned to leave with her.

"Yeah, I got one too. Need to pay the rent and all that."

Jon looked at Belle. "Don't you have a date tonight?"

Belle's eyes narrowed. "And how would you know that?"

"Carlton and I talk."

"Shit." Belle kept her opinions brief. She stomped to the door. "You want a ride, Honey?"

I thought for a millisecond about spending the night with Jon. A Jon-induced orgasm was one of those "Holy shit! What just happened to me?" moments. His big screen TV was pretty good too. But I had some thinking to do about drug-dealing gorillas. Jon was in cop mode anyway and might not be in any other mode even if I did hang around.

I'd joined Belle at the door when Jon spoke again. "Honey?"

I turned, half-hoping he would convince me to stay.

"That guy you brought to the police station? He's officially a homicide. Turf wars are dangerous. Stay out of it."

"Huh. All I do is drive." I followed Belle out the door. By the time we got to Belle's car my hands were shaking.

The reality and finality of death had sunk in. Someone I had contact with was gone, completely. No second thoughts for him, no new life out of jail. I sucked in a deep breath.

"You gonna be okay?" Belle looked at me as she started the car.

"I guess. I didn't know him or care about him, but someone might have. It just seems so arbitrary, to die like that."

"Life is. Arbitrary. Everyone makes choices. His weren't very smart. But you're right, no one deserves what he got." She backed out of the driveway. "Let's make sure we don't make the same stupid choices."

"Luck is a big part of it too. If that bullet had been a little bit to one side, he might have lived and changed his choices. He might have found some people to help him. He might have gotten married, had kids and lived in a house with a white picket fence." I leaned my head back against the seat.

"Uh huh," said Belle and drove off.

She dropped me at my apartment and whizzed down the street to get ready for her date. Belle was good at compartmentalizing. Me? Not so much.

I arrived at Cool Rides at nine o'clock the next morning, extra-large caramel salted, chocolate-sprinkled mocha latte with whip in hand. Mona passed me two fare slips. One was immediate. The other was flexible.

The immediate was a pickup in Holyoke, a larger city to the south and right off the interstate. I passed the big box stores and fast food chains crammed along a five-mile stretch of road and picked her up at a motel on the strip. She looked about thirty, but her skin was wrinkled from years of smoking. She smelled like an ashtray. Her scoop neck tee shirt looked new and her designer blue jeans were properly faded. Her nice new high-tops were red and black with sparkles. But I knew the Goodwill store in town had some pretty good hand-me-downs. Heaving her bag into the back seat, she settled herself in front with a pile of hand-written cardboard signs, each about one foot square.

"I got a change of clothes in the bag." She smiled at me. "Doesn't look good if I'm too dressed up. Like my new shoes? They're on sale at the mall. They are sooo cool, I got 'em in five different colors."

She clicked her seat belt and started shuffling through the cardboard.

"So, let's see. *Pregnant and homeless?* Not cold enough for the *Winter's coming* sign. *Shelter closed for the summer?* No, not sympathetic enough. *Wounded vet, Abused wife, Mother of six?*" She flipped them, rejecting one after the other. "Here, this one's good: *Medicare cancelled my drug money.* Or maybe *Disabled, need beer money.*"

"Where am I taking you?" I grumbled. "And how are you paying?"

"Northampton and cash," she said, pulling out a roll of bills the size of a gorilla's fist. They were all fives and twenties.

"Whoa, you make that panhandling?"

"You bet. It's all cash, no taxes. Just taxis." She burst out laughing at her wittiness. "Maybe I'll move to a better hotel tonight. Gotta stay under the radar though. Wouldn't want the IRS to come sniffin' around my cash flow. That's how they got Al Capone, you know. Income tax evasion."

Wonderful, I was driving Al Capone to collect her daily guilt money. I dropped her at the main

141

intersection in town. The panhandlers divided up the downtown. She had to find her territory before setting up shop. I wondered how she pulled off the pregnant and homeless routine until I saw her open the backpack. She pulled out a round pillow with Velcro straps hanging from it. I guess that was the sign for today. Tomorrow she might be the mother of a newborn.

I sighed and moved on. She had tipped me generously. It was an efficient way to redistribute the wealth. Filter through the rich and guilty to her to me. My personal version of trickle-down economics.

The flexible pick up was at the same motel. As I was pulling over to drop off the first fare, she was calling her significant other and telling him to get his lazy ass out of bed because the taxi would be there in twenty minutes. Apparently panhandlers are like any other professionals and don't embrace the concept of car-pooling. If they did, I would be down one fare so I wasn't complaining.

When I picked up her partner, I noticed he was wearing some pretty nice shoes too. He opened his backpack and replaced them with a pair of ratty sneakers.

"Hey, did Gertrude have all the signs?" he asked.

"She had a bunch of cardboard. I guess it was signs."

"Good, she can be pregnant and homeless today. I'll be a wounded war hero." He paused. "And homeless," he added.

"Are any of you homeless?"

"You mean the panhandlers? Nah. Homeless are in the system. They got a different career path.

142

Housing, meds, looking for a job, working for someone else. Me? I'm self-employed. You get into the system, they got control over you. I'm my own boss."

"Your income is just panhandling? I mean do you have any, like, side jobs?"

"You mean drugs? Illegal stuff? Not much. Too dangerous. I've redistributed a few scrips as a favor for some people. But you gotta be real careful with that stuff. People are territorial. And that bunch, they're violent. Me? I'm a pacifist."

"So, you know who sells stuff like oxycodone around here?"

"You mean where can you get it or who runs the market?"

"I guess who runs things."

"I don't use that stuff so I'm not really sure about who's in charge. But word on the street is that there is some conflict at the moment."

"Conflict?"

"Movement. Someone wantin' to move stuff here from outta town."

"And the people in charge don't want to share?" I asked.

"Guess not. But, like I said, I don't know much about it."

For not knowing much, he was a great source of information for someone as nosy as I am.

I dropped him on Main Street. He was even more generous than Gertrude with his tip. I headed back to the garage. Belle should be in by now and she would be getting the third degree from Mona and Riggs about her date with the judge. I wanted to be in on it.

The only car in the parking lot at Cool Rides was the Stealth Mobile. Willie had added to its lack of appeal by repairing the trunk just enough to be functional but not pretty. Mona sat at her desk fiddling with papers. I assumed Riggs and Belle were out on rides.

"Hey," I greeted Mona. "Where is everyone?"

"Making money. How'd you do with the panhandling population?"

I dumped the cash on the desk. "Interesting couple. Self-employed go-getters."

"Nice tips." She dumped the money in the shared top drawer. Sharing tips made more sense than fighting over the best fares. In the big picture we all made more money when we shared. Too bad the rest of the world didn't see things that way.

I was about to ask Mona if Belle's date had been discussed yet when Riggs and Belle walked through the door laughing. "I couldn't believe she had a real bull-whip with her," said Belle.

"A guy that size? I don't blame her. Evens the odds."

"She really knew how to work that thing."

Belle turned to us. "So, Riggs pulls up in front of me at this big Victorian up on College Hill, lets out the husband, boyfriend, whatever. I'm right behind him with the lady who pops out of my car with a bull-whip coiled and ready. Before we can put the cars in drive, she's flicked him on the butt, right through his Armani suit. And it wasn't a cheap knock-off. Then she coils him up and reels him in with the thing, just like Indiana Jones. I thought they were going to make it right there on the lawn."

"They might have for all we know." Riggs laughed. "We raced each other to get far enough away that we couldn't see what happened."

"Excellent people," said Belle and tossed a fifty-dollar bill on the desk.

"Oooh, the guy wasn't quite as excellent," added Riggs, handing over a twenty.

"Purse strings." Belle sang in a falsetto and danced in a tight circle. "Belong to the woman, especially when she has the whip."

"Excuse me? And who paid for the date last night?" Riggs punched Belle lightly on the shoulder.

"Hey, he invited me. Whoever extends the invitation is responsible for the funding."

"I wonder which one of your couple paid for the whip," I said.

"Mutual benefit, bet they went halvsies," said Belle.

"How was the date? The one with the judge?" I asked.

"Oh, that one. Why? Did you have one too?"

"Not me. I spent the night in my own great company. Alone."

"You should have called me. Henry had night shift at the hospital. I'm good company too," said Riggs.

I looked at Belle. "We seem to be avoiding the subject, which would be the date. Where'd you go?"

"We ate." Belle started out the door.

"Wait!" I trotted after her.

She sat down in a plastic lawn chair and tilted her head back. It was sunny. She closed her eyes.

"Belle, is everything ok?"

145

"Oh, yeah. He took me to a big party at the College Art Museum. We danced, we ate, we made small talk with the big wigs. Then he dropped me off at my apartment."

"So? That sounds great."

"Yeah, he took me out in public. He acts as though I'm normal."

"Uh, huh."

"Well, I'm not. What if he decides to follow a career path?"

"God forbid."

"And he isn't the kind of guy who shares. If I get involved here, its monogamy all the way, Honey. I'm not sure I can handle that."

"Belle, in the two years I've known you, you have had zero relationships. You told me yourself that Big George, the vibrator, was the best sex you were getting."

Belle smiled. "Yeah, I think Carlton might be better than Big George."

"Maybe you should give yourself a chance to find out."

"Yeah, well, Big George doesn't ask for a white picket fence, two and a half kids and a Golden Retriever."

We sat for a few minutes thinking about relationships until Mona called out.

"Excuse me ladies, got fares here. Lucille is ready for the senior center. She's back at Miss Virginia's house but says she has an adequate supply of cookies. Belle? Liquor store run for the Bamstables up on Crescent, and toilet paper for Mr. Steinberg."

146

We left the sunshine and went inside to get fare slips and keys.

Mona handed me my slips and said, "Jon said to tell you both that the home invader guy from Virginia's house was bailed out. So keep your eyes open."

Belle frowned. "What? How'd he get out? He's a menace to society. Being a ho is illegal but guys like that are runnin' around loose. Go figure." She stomped out the door to pick up the Bamstable's daily booze and Steinberg's ass-wiping supplies.

A few minutes later, I parked at the curb in front of Miss V's house. The flowers were still blooming, and Lucille must have watered the potted plants. Nothing was wilted but the house seemed less cheery than before. Maybe it needed its owner home or maybe it was my own frame of mind. Finding out that the idiot home invader had been released hadn't helped my mood. I trotted up the steps and knocked.

"It's open," Lucille's voice sang out.

I was about to step forward when a hand clamped over my mouth and an arm snaked around my body. I tried to scream but only managed a stifled squeak. The attacker shoved me inside and slammed the door. Lucille looked up in surprise.

"Oh dear, and who might you be?" She stumbled back against the counter with her hand to her bosom.

"I'm the guy you don't want to mess with again," he said in a nasal whine.

I recognized the voice of the home invader.

"And I will ask you again, who are you?" asked Lucille.

147

"Gimme the list or I'm gonna shoot this lady full of holes." I saw the gun held at his side.

Lucille continued to rest against the counter. Her right hand was behind her. I squirmed a little and the arm tightened around me.

"Fuckin' hold still," he said.

Lucille took a step forward and the drawer opened mysteriously behind her. I hoped she remembered she wasn't in her house and that drawer wasn't her junk drawer.

"Oh, I'm just so flustered. I don't think I've ever seen such a big gun." Lucille's voice took on the tremor of age. "Please, please don't hurt us." She grabbed her dress at the sides and knotted the fabric in anguish.

I shifted my weight to keep from falling over.

There was a loud bang followed by an earsplitting scream. The arm around me dropped and the body it was attached to fell to the floor writhing in pain. I ducked down and clapped a hand over my ear.

"Oh, just look at this dress now," muttered Lucille. "It was one of my favorites."

There was a bullet hole about a foot above the hem. Lucille turned to the junk drawer and retrieved a roll of duct tape. "Still, not a bad shot," she said.

I guess she had settled into the junk drawer part of Miss V's house. I stood dumbly holding my ear while she bound his hands with the duct tape. She slapped a piece around the leg wound to stop the blood.

"No sense in making a big mess." She stood up. "Honey would you call the police, please? And let us prepare a proper statement for Jon. I'm sure he'll lead the charge." She finished taping and turned to me. "You've been good for him, you know," she said.

"Who?"

"You make him understand that he can't control everything. You are clearly beyond his ability to command," Lucille continued without answering my question.

I wasn't sure if that was true and I couldn't decide if it was good or bad. I was a little woozy, so I hit speed dial for the police. Which, of course, was Jon.

"Jon?" I whispered into my cell.

"Honey? Are you okay?" Jon's voice elevated slightly.

"I'm at Virginia's house. Can you come right away? And maybe bring an ambulance?"

"Shit!" His voice was all the way up now. I heard the thump of feet and the phone went silent.

Minutes later the feet continued thumping up the steps and into the room where I stood staring vacantly at the man on the floor. He must have passed out because he had stopped writhing around. The combination of adrenaline and the absurdity of being rescued by an old lady in a flower print dress ganged up on me. I had a sudden urge to kick something and only resisted the guy lying on the floor because he wasn't moving. I tried to feel sorry for him since he was just bested by an eighty-something year old lady and he did have a bullet in him.

Jon charged through the front door, weapon drawn. I sort of lost my desire to kick things. He took in the situation, holstered his gun and grabbed my arms.

"Are you hurt?"

I shook my head but couldn't stop the tremors. He gathered me in and held me, resting his head on mine. Lucille came over and he pulled her into the embrace. We stood for what seemed like a wonderfully long time.

"You're okay," he muttered into my hair, reassuring both of us even though I knew how I felt. I didn't say anything about kicking bodies.

The EMTs and uniforms arrived, and Jon turned to deal with them.

"At the hospital, on the door, twenty-four," he said to the uniform. Jon wanted this guy watched around the clock.

When all the uniforms and EMTs had left, Jon looked hard at Lucille.

"I know you have a permit for that thing. But I still have to file a report. So, I need to know exactly what happened. And why you have a bullet hole in your dress."

"It was the best shot available at the time. In the heat of the moment, I forgot that I was wearing my favorite dress."

Jon sighed. "Honey?"

"He must have been around the corner of the house. I didn't see him until he was right behind me. They shouldn't have let him out."

"I need to find out who made his bail and why he's so interested in you," said Jon, looking distracted.

Neither Lucille nor I mentioned the list that our attacker had demanded. Jon got a few more details and headed for the station. He asked me to come to his house from work. He thought it would be safer. I didn't see any harm in it and Lucille agreed to spend the night at her house. Apparently, Jon felt better with his womenfolk gathered around him. I snorted and realized that my shakiness had disappeared.

I loaded Lucille and a large supply of cookies into the cab and went to the senior center. As I dropped her off, I noticed a black SUV parked in the lot. Then I looked around and realized there were at least four other black SUVs of various makes parked around the lot. I vowed not to be paranoid. I would check for tinted windows before I threw a stone at any big black vehicles. Then it dawned on me that most official vehicles had tinted windows. What's the world coming to when you can't tell the politicians from the crooks?

By the time I headed back to the garage it was past lunch time, so I called Mona to see if anyone wanted me to pick up take-out. Taco Bell won, and I swung into the drive-thru. I got back to Cool Rides with enough food to last until the next asteroid strikes earth.

"Enough!" Mona patted her stomach and got up to answer the phone.

"Honey? You're up." She handed me three fare slips.

I spent the next four hours driving in circles around town. I understand how race car drivers feel. Lots of driving under lots of stress and going nowhere. Three ladies to a restaurant, three ladies home. Two guys to doctor's appointments, two guys home. I worked my ass off and maybe made a living wage. At least race drivers get paid better. Five more fares from the Survival Center free food distribution to Walmart to subsidized housing. Lugging bags of groceries and enough electronics to confuse an airline pilot was like an hour of lifting weights at the gym. I staggered into Cool Rides. Belle offered me a ride to Jon's.

When we got to his house Belle dropped me and scooted off to another date with Carlton. Jon wasn't home, but I thought I heard him next door at Lucille's. I knocked and listened to the locks click open.

Jon was pacing and talking. "I can't protect you in the middle of an investigation. Because of who you are and what you've done the department is cutting you a lot of slack. But you need to stay out of my way."

He turned to me. "And I found the kid who swapped booze for drugs with Herman. He sold them to, and I quote, 'some old broad.' He claimed she bought drugs all the time. From lots of people."

"Have you found her?" I asked.

"His description was a bit vague."

"How vague?"

"Again, I quote, 'old. They all look the same to me.'"

Terry was sitting in front of Lucille's computer. He had on a new shirt, so he must have spent the afternoon shopping. He didn't seem concerned about the insanity swirling around him, but then, teenagers often live in the moment. Jon's frustration level was showing big time. There were too many people who should be locked up but no real evidence to make it happen. I thought he was about to cross examine Terry when his cell phone rang.

"Stevens," he barked into it.

"Shit," he mumbled a second later. His face clouded over, and he was in full cop mode.

"Jonny, what happened?" Lucille put a protective hand on Terry's shoulder.

152

Jon sighed. "Another body. The idiot you shot just died."

Lucille turned an odd shade of gray. "What?! That was a minor injury. I even taped it to avoid blood loss."

"He didn't die from your gunshot. Asphyxiation. I need to question the officer on guard. Lock up as soon as I'm out the door." Jon closed the door behind him.

Terry got up and started flipping locks.

I turned to Lucille. "Who do you think the old lady drug lord is? Do you know anyone at the senior center who might do something like that for money?"

"Most of my friends are in the bridge groups. All of them are highly competitive and certainly capable of violence. But selling prescription drugs takes contacts. With suppliers and buyers. It would need to be organized."

"What did Jon mean about who you are and what you've done?"

"Oh, I stopped listening after he said something about protecting me. I believe I've told you that I'm a better shot than Jon. And I'm not the shy, retiring type that Ginny Percy is. When is she getting back, by the way?"

"I think Mona said she's scheduled to be picked up in a couple of days."

"Well, I suppose I can maintain her plants for another day. I might restock her kitchen. There is nothing worse than coming home to an empty refrigerator. And her shelves are so bare. I might also look around for lists of things to do at her house." Lucille smiled.

153

I had forgotten about the list that the home invader demanded. Neither of us mentioned it to Jon. Maybe it didn't exist. Maybe Miss V had taken it with her. Maybe it was a map to the female orgasm in which case Jon didn't need it. With that many maybes Jon would only get frustrated trying to figure it out. And maybe I would help Lucille water Miss V's plants tomorrow morning.

Chapter Twelve

The next morning, I had a blessedly normal fare to the airport. A family on their way to Disney World. The trip to Bradley Airport is only forty-five minutes. It was good it wasn't Logan Airport, which is two hours away. The Mouseketeer song is about a minute long and I must have heard it forty times.

On the way back, I passed two eighteen-wheelers hauling telephone poles. They each had an oversized load sign on the back and a chaser car with the same sign. The chaser car was a Mini and it wore its sign with attitude. If I can ever afford a car of my own it will be a Mini Cooper. Belle let me drive hers once. Motoring in a Mini is a great experience.

When I got back to the garage, I was still humming Mickey's song under my breath. Belle pulled in behind me.

"Time to get Lucille," Mona said as I walked through the door.

"She wanted to know when Miss V is coming back. And I want to know if I'm doing the pickup."

"Miss V canceled her pickup. Said she needed to stay away a little longer. She'll call with a new date."

Belle looked confused which is a rare expression for Belle. "I swear I saw Miss V out at the Highway Hotel. She was getting on a bus to the casino along

155

with a few other people of age. Everybody's in a hurry to lose money."

"All I know is she called from Savannah and said she'd let us know when she needed us." Mona turned to me. "After you finish with Lucille, get Meri. She fired another personal care attendant for drinking her special water. So, you're her PCA until she gets a new person from the agency."

That was fine by me. When Meri showed me the matched set of pearl-handled revolvers her late husband gave her, I decided she was a hot ticket. Now she was having memory lapses and I hoped she didn't have any bullets for the guns. Her special water wasn't of the alcoholic kind. It was bottled water that she swore tastes better than anything she ever drank.

Her problem was the same as Herman's had been, but for different reasons. She went through PCAs like water and she went through a lot of water. One of the PCAs used Meri's nap time to watch porn on cable. That worked until Meri got the cable bill. Another had her own version of porn with her boyfriend during Meri's nap time. One didn't like Meri's cat, another reported her to the retirement home director when she left the stove on. They disconnected the stove, but the PCA was history.

The PCA agency had a limited pool of applicants so someone she fired might reappear a month later, hoping she had forgotten either the person or the offense. It had to be pretty serious for the agency to can someone. Being drunk or stoned on the job, or abuse of the patient would be grounds for dismissal. Older people tend to misplace things regularly, so the agency didn't take allegations of theft seriously unless they found the missing item walking out the door with the PCA.

My plan was to take Meri out for lunch and maybe to a museum. That would work if she was up to date on her pain meds. If she forgot to take them, she got cranky or worse. I checked the pill container before I helped her to the car. The space for that day's meds was empty.

"Did you take your pain meds?" I asked her.

"Is it missing?"

"Uh, huh," I said.

"Then I must have taken it."

I could see her logic, so we headed out. Half an hour into the drive, Meri started groaning.

"My knee hurts too much. But Ginny gave me the pain pill. I remember that now. She handed me the pill and said that it would keep me from hurting."

"Ginny?" I assumed that was one of the retirement home nurses who had come by to check up on Meri after the departure of the latest caretaker.

"Virginia. She came by this morning. She heard that I fired that awful PCA person. I don't know where they got her. She just wasn't up to standard."

"Who is Virginia?" I could check with this person and find out if Meri had missed some meds.

"Virginia Percy. You know her from the senior center. She's a friend of Lucille's." Meri shifted in her seat and let out a sound like a wounded puppy. I turned the car around.

"Are you sure that was this morning? I think Miss Virginia is out of town."

"Oh, no! She came to visit early this morning. You can ask the kitchen crew. They let her in after they asked me. I told them it was okay."

Either Meri was confused about when Virginia had visited, or she was hallucinating. Or I wasn't up to date on Virginia's return. But if anyone would know, it would be Mona. I would check with her.

I pulled up to the retirement home, snagged a wheelchair and took Meri to her apartment. On the way to the nurse's office I had to pass the kitchen. I stopped to ask when and who they had let into see Meri.

"Si, an old lady," responded the dishwasher as he hosed breakfast dishes.

"When?"

"Early."

"Early when?" I felt like *who was on first*.

"Early."

"Early today? Yesterday? What day?"

"Early today. An old lady to see an old lady."

"What did the old lady look like?"

"Like the one lives in 6A."

That was Meri. "The other old lady. The one that came to visit. What did she look like?"

"Old."

I went to see the nurse. She promised that she would deal with the prescription problem, so I told Meri to call us when she felt better.

When I got back to Cool Rides, Belle had just pulled in. She was snagging a lawn chair and dragging it out into the sun. "Hey, grab one off." She motioned me to join her.

158

We were comfortably watching the action on the biking, running, see how sore we can make ourselves spandex highway that ran next to the garage when Belle opened one eye.

"Have you seen Miss Virginia?" she asked.

"Not exactly." I explained Meri's meds problem and her thinking that Virginia had been at her apartment.

"Why?" I asked.

"Because Carlton saw her in his courtroom."

"He talks about his cases to you?"

"No, but I picked up the fifteen-year old kid who happened to be the defendant and I happened to give him a ride to the courthouse. Talkative little bugger. He got busted for swiping his grandmother's meds. Told me he got good money for them. Might help pay the rent. The kid told me he knew Virginia and she was there watching him. Carlton just confirmed it."

"And Carlton was sure it was her?"

"Right there in his courtroom during that particular trial. I'm wondering if she really is back and why she didn't call us to pick her up."

"Maybe the trip down was too exciting for her."

"She seemed fine at the time."

"And why would she be in the courtroom?"

We were pondering that when Mona yelled at us. "Got rides here!"

"So Carlton is still on the agenda?" I asked before we were inside.

"We'll talk later. But, yeah, right now he is, I guess."

"Nothing like a rousing endorsement," I mumbled and took the fare slip from Mona's fingers.

Belle grabbed the slip from Mona's other hand and off we went. *Later* turned out to be five trips to the doctor, three movie viewers, one screaming two-year-old to day care, one howling basset hound to the vet and then returning them all to points of origin. When we finally both checked in for the end-of-day settle, we were both too tired to go anywhere interesting.

"Let's go visit Lucille. We can pick up a pizza and see what she made for dessert," groaned Belle.

That was fine by me. I was curious what Lucille was doing with Terry and how her exploration of the supply lines of the local illegal prescription drugs was going. Mona hadn't heard from Miss Virginia, so if she had come back from Savannah, we didn't transport her, which was unusual. Unusual always made me wonder and when I wondered, I needed to know. Lucille was a great source for gossip. Her friends at the senior center talked a lot about everything. And, like me, Lucille could be a good listener. We took Belle's Mini and a pizza to go. On the ride over, we talked about Belle's love life.

"So, still seeing the judge."

"Yup."

"In bed yet?"

"Nope."

And we were there. Small towns can be a drag. We would have to talk later.

"Oh, how lovely!" Lucille greeted us at the door. "That pizza will go perfectly with my new cookie recipe."

I couldn't imagine a good combination of cookies and pizza. Shows what I know.

"How's Terry doing?" asked Belle.

"Oh, he's lovely. He's studying for his GED."

"Hi." Terry emerged from one of the bedrooms. With Lucille's diet of cookies, he had put on a little weight. Or maybe his eyes just didn't have that scared rabbit look anymore. No one from his previous life reported him missing and no one here wondered who he was. But he kept a low profile and Lucille could be a formidable person to challenge if anyone did question the arrival of a new kid in town. Social Services hadn't noticed him and Jon hadn't reported him. So he settled into Lucille's spare room. He could do worse.

His background was still a mystery. I'm not a big fan of mysteries. Where did he go to school? Where had he lived in New York, if that really was where he came from? Inquiring minds needed to know.

"Hey, Terry, how's it hangin'?" I asked.

"Okay, I guess."

I waited until his mouth was full of pizza. "So, you grew up in New York, like on Manhattan?"

"Uh huh," he mumbled through a bite of pepperoni.

"Like, what neighborhood?"

Terry stared at me for a few seconds. Then he stared at the pizza. "Fifth Avenue."

"Pretty uptown."

"Yeah, Fifth Avenue. Nice place."

"It's a long street."

Terry hesitated again. "The four hundred block."

"Near the library?"

"Four fifty-five," said Terry. "My front yard had curb appeal."

"You lived in the library?"

161

"Uh, huh. It's a big place."

Lucille was busy at the kitchen sink. I suspected she'd already heard some of this story.

"When I was five, my mother disappeared. We were living in an abandoned building. Even the police didn't go in there. I figured anyplace was safer, so I moved. I'd been to the library once and it seemed like a nice place."

"How did you eat?"

"We are talking New York City, right?" Teenage scorn was back. "I figured out when the good restaurants tossed the best stuff. I showed up and ate like Donald Trump."

"Where'd you go to school? I mean, you can read and do math, right?"

"Duh! I lived in the New York City Library for ten years. I found out they have showers, a workout room, a bunch of kitchens, offices with beds. They have reading hours, help with homework, and online classes. I read The Catcher in the Rye when I was ten. Holden Caulfield, what a whiner." He shrugged like it was normal for a ten-year-old kid to read J.D. Salinger.

The New York Public Library was his home base for ten years. I had just met the real-life Librarian. I had a brief stint in the homeless category and I had to give the kid credit. Moving into such posh digs was a brilliant move.

"What did you do for money?"

"I ran errands for people. When I got older, I did babjs for cash."

"Babjs?"

"Back alley blow jobs. That's how I met the gorilla guy. He told me that he had some opportunities outside the city, so I figured, why not?"

"What did he say they were?"

"Nothing special, just stuff."

I tried to think. Like what made this guy zero in on Northampton. Why would he think there would be a profit here? I had brain freeze. Nothing was making sense to me.

I envisioned someone on a loud speaker. "Brain freeze on aisle ten." Terry's story about his childhood had blown my brain onto the planet Bob.

I decided to take a break from worrying about someone else and worry instead about where I would spend the night.

"Remember I need a ride first thing in the morning, dear. I must be on time." Lucille delicately sliced off a bite of pizza.

That settled the *where* question. I finished my pizza, grabbed cookies to go and said goodnight to Lucille and Terry. Belle left with me and headed to her car.

Jon wasn't home, so I used my key and crashed in his bedroom.

I woke up the next morning with a hairy male leg draped over my hip and something nudging me from behind. I was thinking about helping the nudge along when the alarm on my phone went off.

Jon pulled a pillow over his head and rolled over. The nudging disappeared.

I staggered to the shower.

Ten minutes later I knocked on Lucille's door.

"Oh good, you're a bit early. We can stop for coffee on the way."

I zipped up Main Street to the first coffee shop, Sip and Suck. I pulled in a few spaces behind a new Land Rover. There were two men standing in the empty space between, watching the Rover. One of them leaned against the parking meter, the other leaned on a baseball bat pointed into the pavement. An overly well-dressed guy wandered out of the coffee shop and pushed the alarm button off. The big vehicle beeped and blinked.

"This yours?" asked the guy with the bat.

"Yeah, ain't she a looker?" The car guy had gold chains around his neck and looked like a regular at a tanning salon. Somehow, despite his expensive clothing, he exuded slime.

"Oh yeah." The guy raised the bat to his shoulder. His companion backed up a step. I stayed in my car.

"Your name God?"

"I know you?"

"You know my kid. He calls you Guaranteed Overnight Delivery."

"Yeah." The guy with the gold grinned widely. "That's where the God comes from."

"You delivered some stuff to my kid," said Mr. Bat and swung with all the force in his well-developed biceps. The Rover's back window shattered. He worked his way around the car turning each window into a pile of glittering peas. When he finished, he grabbed Rover guy by the gold, pulling his face close.

"You ever sell that stuff to my kid again..." He paused, tightening his hold. "This here bat will hit a home run with your head. Foosh!!" He gestured with

164

his free hand. "Right over centerfield. Out onto the parking lot. Splat! Got it?" They were nose to nose when the father muttered, "His name? Always remember John Smith. Anyone under the age of twenty is called John Smith and you won't be selling drugs to any of them."

Mr. God's head bobbed wildly. Some big city drug dealers are tough and usually carry a variety of weapons. Not so much in towns like Northampton. Mr. Bat and his friend drove off. God stood looking morosely, and a bit uncertainly, at his car.

"Well, I'm ready for coffee," said Lucille cheerfully and got out of the taxi. She walked over to the windowless car. "I guess he didn't share your religious views, dear." She strolled to the coffee shop.

I heard sirens approaching. The squad car and the bicycle cop arrived at the same time. It took the cops less than a minute to get to the scene. That was after someone finally called them. Most of the locals knew where the owner of the Rover got enough money to buy his car, his gold chains and his tanning time. They were cheering for the baseball bat.

Rover guy was putting it in gear when the cops asked him to step out of his windowless car. Glass pebbles covered the pavement around his parking space.

"You gonna clean up this mess?" one of the cops asked him, leaning on the driver's side window hole.

"My girlfriend's ex," he said, as if that explained everything.

"Uh huh. You gonna clean it up?" the cop repeated.

The other cop walked over to my car.

165

"See anything?"

"Maybe a drug deal gone bad?" I said.

"Yeah, I guess," he said and returned to his patrol car to radio in.

Someone came out of the coffee shop with a broom and dustpan and handed it to Mr. Rover. The cops planted themselves on the sidewalk and watched as he started slowly pushed the broken glass into a pile.

Lucille came out and slid into my passenger seat. "I wouldn't guess he's going to press charges," she said.

I dropped Lucille off at the dentist with the promise to return in an hour and take her to Miss Virginia's house to water the plants.

When I pulled into Cool Rides the cars were getting washed. We hadn't had any more drive-by shootings so maybe the idiots in big, black SUVs were focused on someone else. Like whoever was running the business they seemed to want to take over.

"Hey." Belle came over as I picked up the vacuum and started detailing the last car in line. "How's the judge?"

"Humph," Belle grunted. "We're going to a play tonight."

"Whoa! How many dates does that make?"

"Maybe we can double. Carlton and Jon can talk shop and we can listen."

"We can solve cases for them."

"Tell them how to judge."

"How to chase bad guys."

"Plenty of those to go around."

"Yeah, but I haven't seen any today."

"Watch yo' mouth. Don't tempt the fates."

Belle and I were laughing when Mona yelled out, "Lucille!"

"I have been summoned," I said. I grabbed the gas card off Mona's desk. I knew the tank was low. I could fill it after I finished with Lucille.

I picked Lucille up and we headed over to Virginia's house to do a plant watering and general check. Lucille had decided to keep an eye on the place until Miss V returned, whenever that might be.

Some of the plants on Virginia's porch were wilted. There was a general unoccupied and neglected feel to it that I didn't remember. The grass on the tiny lawn was taller. Some of it had gone to seed. It would be good for Miss V to come home.

We climbed the steps and I bent down to touch a wilted leaf. It felt limp between my fingers. I took the last step and realized that the front door was ajar. Lucille's hand went into her oversized pocketbook. I remembered that she had purchased one of the light weight guns from the Pretty in Pink line. It was much easier to carry than the Glock. She looked over and motioned me away from the door. She stepped to the side and nudged it farther open. The gun was in her hand but still down at her side. When the gun went up and she assumed her 007 stance, I knew enough to duck and run.

The door swung open. We both peeked around the door jamb and saw a figure in the kitchen. Lucille's gun hand came up. She stiffened her back and extended her arm, turning sideways to provide a smaller target. I backed up. The figure turned toward us.

"Virginia? What in God's name are you doing here?" Lucille's hand disappeared back into her bag.

"Oh!" Miss Virginia Percy let out a surprised yelp.

That solves the mystery of where Miss V is, I thought.

"I live here. What are you doing here?"

"Watering your flowers, which, I might add, could really use some attention." Lucille walked over to the counter and dropped her bag.

"Well, I can do that now. Thank you for worrying about them."

"I didn't worry about them. It just seemed a waste to let them all die and you didn't see fit to let us know that you had returned." Lucille put some steel in her voice.

"Well, I'm here now and I have some pressing engagements." Virginia looked around as if her engagements should press pretty soon.

I watched in fascination as the two elderly ladies faced each other.

Suddenly Lucille's body language changed. "Ginny, why didn't you call us? Is there a problem? Is your family okay?" Lucille became the sympathetic older sister.

"Everyone is fine. I just have some private matters that I must attend to. So, you should probably leave."

That made me curious. What private matters would an elderly lady like Virginia have that she obviously didn't want to share? She didn't want us to wait while she took care of something. She wanted us gone. I had a strange feeling. If Lucille hadn't been standing next to me, I would have been gone.

The two women had achieved a two-sided checkmate when Miss V's landline rang.

Chapter Thirteen

The person on the other end was screaming loud enough for all of us to hear. Miss V held the phone an inch away from her ear. "Henry, calm down."

"Well, thank God you're back! We was all wondering how we was gonna make it to the next check. It ain't easy, you know."

"Yes, but, Henry, I must call you back later. I promise I'll take care of everyone soon. Right now I have to get some business straightened away."

"It's gotta be soon though. Like sometime today. Everyone is upset. And they take it out on me."

Virginia put the phone back in its cradle. She turned to us. "Some people become very dependent. I just need to distance myself sometimes."

I had heard that from more than one Personal Care Attendant. I was surprised that Virginia Percy would take on that roll with other elders. PCAs frequently needed to physically help their charges and Miss Virginia was nowhere near strong enough to do that. But maybe her role was more of an emotional type of support. Loneliness is a major problem for the elderly and banding together to provide social contact would make sense. Maybe Miss V was the organizer. That wasn't quite the vibe I had picked up from the phone screamer, but what did I know? I didn't want to overreact to something as innocent as a lonely old man.

"I need to use the little lady's room," said Miss V and went into the bathroom. We heard the lock click closed.

I was considering what my other questions might be when we heard the soft thunk of a car door closing. Lucille turned to look out the window when the door burst open.

A man with an oversized bandage on his pinky finger stood pointing a gun at us. The bandaged pinky might be a liability when it came time to aim the gun, but I decided not to risk it. His bulk blocked the doorway, but I recognized the feet behind him. He stepped inside. Bubba from the Guns and Daisies store stood behind him. He had the same ratty sandals on his feet, but his right foot was wrapped in its own oversized bandage. The grown up Bobbsey Twins, Hardy Boys…no, Curley and Mo. All they needed was a third stooge.

"Grab Granny and let's get out of here."

"What about the broad that drives the taxi?" asked Bubba.

"Yeah, she might know something. And she seen us now. Take her too." He looked at me. "Wait. Pat them down first."

"Huh?" Bubba turned awkwardly.

"Make sure she don't have weapons. Sometimes taxi drivers around here carry."

Bubba grinned and came over to me. He ran his hands over my body suggestively. He found my car keys in my pocket. My cell phone was in my purse, which was on the counter with Lucille's overstuffed bag.

"What you want to do with these?" He held up the keys.

"We'll take the taxi too. Hide it. So they don't know she's missing for a while."

Like that would throw Mona off the track. She would hunt down the car like it was the last transport out of the apocalypse. Me, she might assume I had just gone off to have some personal time. So stealing the car was a good thing from my point of view.

"Search the old lady too."

"Me?" Bubba sounded startled.

"Sometimes old people carry crazy stuff. I heard you get paranoid in your old age."

"Me? I ain't paranoid. I know when someone's lookin' for me. Most of the time." Bubba looked over at Lucille, clearly not wanting to be grouped in the age-related paranoia club.

"Just search her."

"The old lady? She could be my grandma. I don't wanna touch her. I never liked my grandma. She always tried to hug me. Ick!" Bubba backed away from Lucille.

"Jesus! How could you not like your own grandma? Grandmas are sacred." He glanced down at his bandaged finger. "I bet this one don't got no kids. She ain't nobody's granny. Here, hold the gun." He handed the gun to Bubba and started to pat down Lucille. His hand ran down both sides of her body and sort of patted the inside of her legs through the long skirt she was wearing. His bandaged finger kind of made the whole operation awkward and probably somewhat, but apparently not entirely, useless.

"Take it off," he said, backing up. He took the gun and pointed it at Lucille.

"Oh, very well." Lucille yanked up her skirt, unbuckled the holster and gun from her thigh and handed it to him. Lucille had learned something from the last incident where she had to shoot someone. The holster was a swivel design so one could fire the gun without removing it. "Are we done now? What do you want from us?"

I had never seen Lucille's legs above mid-calf. I was impressed.

"We're taking you somewhere where they won't hear so much noise and it won't make so much of a mess. You're gonna tell us all about this thing you got goin'. Now outside."

He pointed at me. "You drive. You do anything funny and Granny here gets a bullet in her brain." He turned to Bubba, the grandma-hater. "Get those blindfolds. We don't want them to know where we're taking them. Just in case."

I stared at him. Okay, I.Q. south of zero. "Excuse me. You want me to drive? Is that with or without the blindfold?"

He stared back at me. Then he stared at the taxi. Then he stared at the black SUV.

"We'll come back for the other car. After we get what we need. I'm gonna call the boss, tell him we got the old lady," he said.

Bubba was still mumbling about his grandmother.

And what about the taxi driver, I thought. How important am I? Maybe the blindfolds were a good idea. The less they thought I knew, the better the odds of surviving Tweedle Dumb and Tweedle Dumber. Jon told me that the reason the cops catch criminals is that the good guys are marginally smarter than the bad guys. He said that after one of his patrol officers had neglected to call in a license plate before he helped someone change a flat. The guy had just held up a Dunkin Donuts where he got $5.31 and a dozen Boston cremes. He gave the officer six of the donuts before he drove off with the spare tire from the police cruiser.

These bad guys were busy proving Jon right.

"Put your hands out," said the fingerless wonder. He fastened a pair of handcuffs that looked like they came from the local porn store over my wrists. They were fuzzy and purple. I wondered if there was a quick release on them.

One of them got a couple of black strips of cloth that looked like they were designed for a Halloween pirate costume. There's a reason professional kidnappers use hoods. You can always see something through a blindfold, even if it's just the floor. I knew the floor of the cab pretty well since I vacuumed it daily. So I looked up and, of course, could see right through the folded black material.

They loaded us into the back of the taxi and we headed out with one driving and the other holding a gun on us, which we presumably couldn't see.

The question now was how long it would take Mona to miss one of her cars. I knew she had some sort of tracking device on them besides the GPS. I had been held at gunpoint once before and she swore that from then on she would know where every one of her cars was 24/7. I didn't know where they were taking us or what they wanted to know, but I would be happy to tell them anything that would keep that gun from going off, either on purpose or by accident.

Virginia hadn't come out of the bathroom while we were being held at gunpoint. I wondered if she heard the conversation and decided to wait until everyone left to come out and call the police. Or if she was too deaf to hear it and would think we had left her alone to water her plants. I was sort of sorry she hadn't come out with guns blazing. Then we would all have been on our way home. If she had a gun. If she knew how to use it. If she had decent aim. And if she was actually on our side. A lot of *ifs*.

We headed south toward Holyoke. We came to one of the neighborhoods that Willie absolutely refused to send any of his drivers to when the car started to stutter. It gave a last shudder and stopped in front of a five-story residential. On one side of the building was a warehouse with sagging metal doors and mostly smashed windows. On the other side was an empty lot filled with rubble from other buildings and a pile of bloated green trash bags. In the middle of the vacant lot was a Lazy Boy recliner with its extension out. It looked like it was sitting in judgment on the city. It was hard to tell if anyone was brave enough to live in the building. I thought I saw a shadow move across one of the windows. It wasn't very clear, given that I still had the stupid blindfold over my eyes.

"What the fuck?" said Bubba, who had the task of driving to the navigation of Mr. Fingers. Apparently, they didn't know how to put the address in the GPS

175

because they had been arguing about how to get where they didn't know they were going. Now it didn't matter because they weren't going to get there on an empty gas tank anyway.

Fingers got out of the car. He raised the hood and poked a few things, jumping back and shaking his hand when it hit a hot spot. I didn't mention the gas gauge as being the first thing I would check.

"I don't know what the fuck's the matter with this piece of shit."

Bubba looked at the surrounding landscape.

Fingers kicked the tire of the stalled car. He stalked back and forth. Then he pulled out his gun and pointed it at the hood of my taxi.

"Don't…" I choked on my words as he pulled the trigger.

The bullet ricocheted off the car and shot through the only unbroken windowpane in the five-story walk-up. The combination of gunshot and breaking glass caused an instant reaction from the residents of all the surrounding buildings, most of which were boarded up and falling down. All of which had a whole lot more than one person inside.

Everything short of a grenade launcher appeared in the rest of the shattered and shuttered windows. Lucille and I dove out opposite sides of the taxi and ran into a narrow alley between two of the dilapidated buildings. Just as we made cover, I noticed a grenade launcher and revised my opinion of the firepower about to let loose. Bubba and Fingers must have appraised it as well because they started running down the street as fast as someone with missing digits could hobble.

Lucille and I pressed against the brick, out of sight of the local militia. We were contemplating our situation when we heard the *crash, fawhump* of the grenade launcher. The Lazy Boy exploded in a shower of foam, brown corduroy, and two-by-fours. The taxi remained remarkably untouched after Finger's first act of stupidness.

"What should we do now?" I asked Lucille, believing her vast experience with law enforcement would be valuable. Our captors had fled but I had no idea how to get out of this neighborhood and into one of the nicer ones that Holyoke had on the other side of the city.

Lucille popped the purple cuffs off her wrists, snapped them closed again, handed them to me, and unbuttoned the top button of her blouse. I thought that rearranging my boobs wouldn't have been a big priority under the circumstances. She reached into her bra and I remembered the bra holster she had purchased at Guns and Daisies.

"We'll be fine." She drew the small but lethal gun from between her breasts and stepped out onto the sidewalk. "I think we should follow those two criminals and see where they lead us."

She started walking in the direction Bubba and Fingers had run like the banshee was on their tails. I looked for the instant release on the fuzzy cuffs. "Ah, Lucille? Could you give me a lesson in dominatrix?"

Lucille turned, rolled her eyes and pushed something on the cuffs which popped open. I was about to toss them in the alley but thought better of it and tucked them in my back pocket. Who knows what Jon might like?

I noticed that Lucille had tucked her cuffs in the elastic of her skirt waistband. With her gun out and handcuffs ready, she was set to deal with anything that came along. The nearby residents either found her not worth their while or completely crazy and therefore possibly dangerous. She was armed with a pink gun and purple handcuffs. That would give most people pause.

It only took us a block to catch up with Bubba. His missing toe and the oversized bandage hampered his speed in escaping the volatile side of town. Mr. Fingers, although not as good a shot with his gun as he might have been, was not similarly encumbered by his wound. He had left Bubba to his own devices and fled as fast as his two good feet could carry him. Bubba was crouched on the front stoop of an unoccupied commercial building. The full front plate glass windows had been blown out from the inside and the shelves that might have once housed the basics of human consumption were scattered across the floor like pick-up-sticks. Gone were the Twinkies, chips, Cheez Whiz, and Wonder Bread of the urban diet.

Bubba swayed back and forth, muttering to himself. As we got closer, I could make out the words.

"My toes hurt, my toes hurt, my toes hurt. Goddamn fuckin' toes." He was repeating this over and over. When he saw us a wave of anger passed over his face. I didn't see any guns, so I figured the fingerless wonder had not only deserted his comrade but taken their only defense with him.

"Hey, Bubba. Where's the rest of the team?" I asked.

"My name ain't Bubba. It's Winfred."

178

"Winfred?"

"Yeah, what about it?"

I looked at the yellowed bandage. Some blood had leaked through and the combination of pus yellow and red wasn't promising.

"You should get that foot checked out."

"It's your fault. Well, it's really her fault." He pointed to Lucille.

"Young man, you drew a knife on me. Did you expect me to fall in a feminine faint?"

"Huh?" Bubba had no idea what Lucille was talking about. He lived in a simple world that probably didn't include the intricacies of women fainting.

We paused long enough with Winfred/Bubba moaning to draw an audience. A couple of tough-looking teenagers with low slung jeans and five-hundred-dollar sneakers were edging closer. A wounded man, an old lady and an unarmed female looked like easy pickings. The two teens got within ten feet. Lucille raised her gun and whistled a shot close to the front runner's ear. The gun was small but accurate and residents of this city knew their weapons. They backed off and faded into the alley.

"Where were you and the fingerless wonder going?" Lucille asked.

"Like I might tell you." Bubba/Winfred/Toes glanced around. "Shit, I could really use a drink. Ya know, just to kill the pain."

"We'll just have to pursue Mr. Fingers further." Lucille started walking up the deserted street. A few faces appeared in the cracked windows of the building across the street.

"Hey, you can't just leave me here! I can't walk and I ain't got nothing to protect me."

"He has a point," I said. I thought Winfred might actually know enough to be worth hauling along with us. I could see the neon sign for a gas station and liquor store a block up. The neon was lit up, so I figured they were in business which meant we might also be back in business. "We could buy a can of gas and go get the taxi."

"Get a bottle of beer while you're there. Better, get some Jack or Jim. My old friends, Jack Daniels and Jim Beam," Winfred muttered to himself.

Lucille stuck her hand into her bra again and came up with a Visa card. "Never travel without the necessities of life. Weapons and plastic," she said and stomped off up the block. I stood wondering what any men who got to first base thought when they found that stash.

"Come on," I said to Winfred. "We can take you to the hospital or something." *Maybe the vet,* I thought. By the time I got him to his feet and hobbling back to the taxi, Lucille had returned and passed us with a full gas can and no booze. We shuffled and staggered to the taxi where Lucille emptied the gas can and was trying to convince the engine to turn over.

Winfred/Bubba leaned against the car, taking weight off his foot, continuing to mutter about his alcoholic needs.

Lucille flipped the key back and forth a few times and the car roared to life.

Winfred slid into the back seat. I guessed we were taking him home with us. It was too late to try to catch up with Fingers anyway.

We drove back to the gas station with me at the wheel. Lucille rode shotgun with her spare gun out and ready should Winfred decide to assert himself. I had no idea where she kept that one.

After filling the tank using Lucille's charge card, we headed back to Northampton.

Lucille turned around to face the back seat.

Winfred shrank down.

"So, who's your boss and what does he want?"

"Lady, all I do is muscle. They said get the old lady, so I went where they told me and I got you. Isn't my fault the cab didn't have any gas. And you ask too many questions. And no booze? What's with that? You were right there at a liquor store," he said resentfully.

I stopped at the traffic light in the center of Northampton. Winfred tried to get the door open. Due to foolish people doing exactly that at high speeds, the car companies have made it very difficult to jump out of a moving car.

"Jesus fucking Christ, I need a drink. Lemme outta here." He started banging on the door and yanking the door handle.

I didn't want to explain a missing door handle to Mona and I was getting sick of hearing about Winfred's alcoholic needs so I put the car in park, and the door popped open. Winfred jumped out just as the light turned green. His movement was constrained by his swollen foot. He also misjudged the closeness of the vehicle in the next lane. It rumbled forward like a greyhound, which is what it was, right over Winfred's other foot. He gave the bus driver a one-finger salute and the side-view mirror from the next car in line clipped the offending finger.

"Oh, just keep going. He isn't going to give us any good information," said Lucille. "We need to swing by Virginia's house to pick up my bag and have a talk with her. Then we can get back to my house and see if Terry has made any progress on his GED studies. And you had better call Mona and thank her for letting you take me to the mall in Holyoke."

We left Winfred hopping around in the middle of the street, horns blaring, people blessing him with creative curses. No one stopped to help him out of the street but they hadn't run over him, either.

Lucille handed me a fifty-dollar bill. She apparently didn't want the afternoon's adventure discussed at the taxi garage or with the police. Okay with me. I'm not all that good at sharing.

We got to Virginia's house and it was locked up and empty. Miss V was nowhere in sight. Her plants hadn't been watered. Even the colorful pots looked forlorn with the dying plants. It also meant she had left in a rush.

"Well, I certainly hope she has a good reason for letting those poor plants die such ignominious deaths," said Lucille, picking up the watering can and taking the key from beneath one of the blighted plants. She unlocked the door just as the phone rang.

Chapter Fourteen

Our oversized bags were upended on the floor. Lucille answered the phone.

"Oh, thank God you're there! We got the money. Thank you sooo much." A female voice just short of hysteria screamed out of the phone.

I looked at my bag. The wallet was open. My cash stash was gone. One advantage to not having a credit card is not having a credit card. It can't be stolen. Lucille's wallet was in similar condition. All the cash was gone. I now knew that she kept her credit card and a spare fifty-dollar bill with her gun in her bra holster. Anything she kept in her wallet was history.

"You're welcome," said Lucille and hung up.

"I think the fingerless wonder might have come back for Virginia and taken the money too," I said, starting to pick up my belongings. "I hope she's okay."

"Why did they call here?" asked Lucille.

"What?"

"That phone call. It was Ginny's land line. Why would someone call thanking her for money right now?"

"Because she came back and paid off some debt?" I asked, looking at my empty wallet.

"Well, let's get the plants watered and get back to my house." Lucille got that empty look that some might interpret as old age or scatter-brained. I knew her brain was busy sorting something out.

When we got to Lucille's half of Jon's house, Terry was at the kitchen table reading the study guide for the Massachusetts GED. A copy of Howard Zinn's History of America was next to him.

"Hey Terry, how's it going?"

"Grown-ups are so dumb."

Ah, the teenager was back.

I watched Terry and Lucille go back and forth about the stupidity of adults and the testing process for high-school graduation. I realized that, if Terry's statement about his background were true, he and Lucille had some pretty big challenges ahead that went beyond the fact that a few drug pushers were interested in giving Terry regular, or not so regular, employment. He had existed outside the system for his entire life. For whatever reason, Lucille had become his guardian, in real time if not legally. How could they legalize that kind of relationship when Terry didn't exist in the system? He had no identity and a most amazing identity at the same time. He had more street experience and possibly more academic knowledge than much of the adult population of the world. And who knew how old he really was? He didn't.

Everything about him was ambiguous, from his sexual orientation, his age, his very existence. His go-with-the flow approach had served him well outside the system, but inside, it might be different.

"I think I should go to the local library." Terry looked at Lucille. I didn't know if Lucille even knew where the local library was.

"You know, we have five college libraries within a half hour. Maybe you should check them out," I said.

"Why don't you drop Terry off at the Northampton library? I assume we have one." Lucille turned to me.

"Okay. Are we still worried about the ape man? Those guys seem to have refocused on the elder end of their drug cartel." At the same time, I didn't want Terry in harm's way.

"I think they're currently looking at the supply end rather than the sales end of their business. That would be the population with the most access to the oxy drugs. That would be the elderly. Which is why we were taken for such a rude ride."

"What ride?" Terry looked puzzled.

"We had a mishap with the taxi. Resulting in more small appendages being injured." Lucille smiled her vacant smile.

"Wait. Who took you for a ride?" Terry looked nervous.

"Someone who is now missing more toes." Lucille continued to smile.

"Hey, I don't want anything happening to you because of some stupid thing I did," said Terry.

"Terry, dear, you are neither the center of the world nor the cause of any of this chaos. It is a hard lesson to learn, but you are just a minor pawn in the game for some very evil people." Lucille was beginning to sound very maternal and Terry had discovered someone he gave a shit about. That must have been a shock to him. But Lucille was right about the teenager's view of their place in the universe. And about the reality of that place. I also figured she was right about the current focus of the idiot drug dealers. Terry was the least of their concerns.

"Come on, I'll drop you at our city library. Don't laugh at the size. And it doesn't have showers or an indoor tennis court." I needed to get back to Cool Rides and start making a living. Lucille needed to bake cookies to get her Zen on. Terry could study at the library.

"Call me when you need to be picked up." I figured I could spend a nice night at Jon's house anyway.

I dropped Terry off at the small-town library. He looked bewildered.

"This is nice," he said hesitantly.

I grinned and left him to sort out small-town living.

When I got to Cool Rides, Mona looked the car over carefully but didn't comment on the length of time I was gone. That was because I handed her Lucille's final tally which was $150.

"There's a message for you to call Lt. Jon at his office." She looked at me as though I might give her some insight about whether this had to do with my slut shoes or my driving.

"Probably wants to have pizza and cannolis tonight. He has really great cannolis. Any fares for me?" I would put off calling Jon as long as possible. I found that discussing anything with Jon was better done in person.

"You can pick up Meri in an hour. She needs some grocery shopping and a trip to the liquor store." Mona handed me the slip.

I was about to start detailing the car when my phone rang. It was Jon.

"Hi, Jon."

"I just got a call from Holyoke. They have a body. Someone saw a Cool Rides taxi three blocks from the kill site. What the fuck is going on?"

"Hi, how are you Jon?"

"It's a dead body, Honey. Did you go to Holyoke today?"

"I took Lucille to the mall. Maybe they saw us there."

"I don't think so."

"Who was the dead guy?"

"He was missing both his little fingers. One had been shot off pre-mortem within the last 36 to 48 hours. The other was cut off and stuffed up his nose. He was sitting in a recliner in an empty lot, buck naked."

I gulped and thanked God or whoever that Jon couldn't see my face. Fingers was a nasty person but I didn't wish him dead in what I was pretty sure was an ugly way. Apparently the residents of Holyoke had an unending supply of disposable recliners because the last one I saw in a vacant lot was in so many small pieces it wouldn't have held a tiny rodent, let alone a human rat.

I needed to talk to Lucille. Maybe it was time to bring Jon up to speed. Maybe Jon had figured out enough to do something. What cops could do and what civilians could do were very different. Sometimes that was good, sometimes not. Lucille and I didn't have to worry about search warrants, but we did have to worry about bad guys with big guns. Lucille maybe less than me because, like the cops, she had her own big gun.

"I thought I might come over for pizza tonight," I said to Jon in as normal a voice as I could muster, trying to distract him.

"Apparently he made the mistake of shooting into a vacant building which wasn't so vacant. He winged a big guy in one of the Holyoke gangs. You know anything about that?"

"Those gang guys are tough. And they don't like to be shot at," I said, thinking that no one likes to be shot at, but not everyone can seek that kind of revenge. Personally, I wouldn't have done the finger thing. It seemed like overkill. "Should I pick up the pizza tonight, or are you working late?"

Jon couldn't tear his focus from Finger's murder. "We will talk about this later." He had that authoritative tone that I so loved to hate.

I hung up. Maybe we would, maybe we wouldn't.

Tonight came pretty fast because I spent the day transporting Meri, whose daughter was staying with her for a week. She seemed better. Maybe the daughter had straightened out the meds.

When I got back to Jon's house, he was next door with Lucille.

I joined him at the table.

Lucille was pacing between the counter and the window. "Did Terry call you to be picked up? Did you forget him?" She looked at me.

"I never got a call and neither did Mona. Maybe he's still at the library."

"The library closed an hour ago."

"So maybe he decided to walk home." It said something to me that I thought of Lucille's house as Terry's home. They had bonded in a very short time.

"Not after our morning discussion."

"Your comment about rude rides? You still think he feels responsible for what happened?"

"What happened?" Jon turned to Lucille.

"We accidentally went to Holyoke. A less than desirable area of the city."

"Accidentally?" Jon turned to me.

"We were sort of kidnapped by Fingers and Toes," I said.

"Kidnapped? Sort of?" Jon's voice was rising a little.

"Who the hell are Fingers and Toes?"

"Toes is a guy who had his little toe shot off. Fingers is missing a finger...or two."

"The dead body in Holyoke." Jon pushed back from the table.

"Oh my," said Lucille innocently. "Did someone give Mr. Fingers a taste of his own medicine?"

"Jesus Christ! What the fuck?" Jon was trying not to yell. "I need you to tell me everything that happened and exactly what these two guys said to you. And why the hell they took you anywhere."

I looked to Lucille. "I think Jon might be able to help if Terry is in trouble. He can find out who people are faster than we can." Except for Mona and her computer. She might leave Jon in the dust.

"When we went to Virginia's house today, several horrid men accosted us with weapons, demanding that we accompany them to a place where they were going

189

to ask us some questions. Apparently one of them didn't survive."

"The car made it up the interstate, but when we got off in Holyoke, it ran out of gas. Fingers got really mad. He shot the car and the bullet ricocheted into the closest building. I guess there were some gang members inside. When they started returning fire, Fingers and Toes took off up the street."

Lucille took up the story. "Toes hates his grandmother, so he missed my bra holster when he searched me. I think Fingers was just in a hurry. There is no excuse for a sloppy search, in my opinion."

Jon stared at her. "Your bra holster?"

Lucille turned from the window and drew the gun from her chest, carefully pointing it at the floor.

Jon ran a hand over his face. I couldn't tell if he was trying not to smile or scream. "So, you were armed when you ended up stranded in Holyoke. How did you get back here?"

"We hiked a block, following Fingers and Toes to see where they went. We found Toes because he couldn't keep up with Fingers. There was a gas station right there, so Lucille bought gas and we drove back to Northampton. Toes decided to come with us but he was having some alcohol related withdrawal problems. He jumped out of the car and a bus ran over his other foot. Then a car might have broken his finger. Then we left and came back to water Virginia's plants."

"You say all this like it's a normal thing. Then you went back to work? Just like that?" asked Jon.

"Well, yeah. There wasn't anything else to do."

"How about call the police? Report that there are guys running around with guns."

"Oh, now, Jonny," said Lucille. "You know you can't do anything without corroborating witnesses. No one saw any of this. And we were both in better shape than either of the kidnappers. But now I'm worried they might have Terry. I think we should focus on that."

"Tell me exactly what they said. We have a better chance of figuring out anything if we know why they're interested in you."

"Well, it was Lucille they were interested in. I was just in the way, I guess."

Lucille looked at me. "No, it was the old lady. Toes said 'I'm just muscle. I went where they told me, and I got the old lady.' I'm an old lady."

"Virginia!" Lucille and I said in unison.

"We need to get over to Ginny's house," said Lucille, snatching her bag off the counter. I wondered what she had restocked in it.

"Will someone clue me in? Please?" said Jon.

"On the way. We need your undercover car. No sirens."

We all got in Jon's car and he drove toward Virginia's house.

"To someone of Fingers' and Toes' mental capacity, all old people look alike. Once your hair turns white, you become just like every other white-haired person. They couldn't tell the difference between me and Virginia. So they took the first white-haired woman they found in the right place. They never asked who I was. They just assumed I was whoever they were supposed to get. I still don't know

191

why they would want Virginia. And she is back in the area, by the way."

"Terry was supposed to help distribute prescription drugs to local teenagers. Maybe Virginia was going to be one of his sources. She takes an oxy drug of some sort," I added.

We had reached Virginia's street and Jon slowed the car. There were no cars in front of the house and no evidence of anyone home. The plants looked marginally better for the earlier watering. He parked a half-block away and we walked to the house. The door was unlocked. Jon motioned us to the side as he drew his weapon. Lucille already had her small gun out of the bra holster. Jon nudged the door. It creaked open. In five minutes, we had determined that no one was there. We were back in the entry area when the phone rang. Lucille walked over and picked it up.

"This is the Percy residence," she said, with a hint of southern drawl that made her sound like Virginia.

"Where the fuck you been? We been calling all day. People count on that money, ya know. It ain't like we can get to the end of the month without it."

"Where did you want me to deliver the money? I can get it to you tonight if you give me the address."

"Same place as always. Nothin's changed. You just be there tonight."

The phone clicked, and Lucille returned it to its cradle. "I don't think that had anything to do with Terry," said Lucille.

The phone rang again. Lucille picked it up.

"Hey, your customers gave me this number. I got something you want. And I want the list of those customers that you got. Listen to this." The voice sounded vaguely familiar. I had only heard Ape man say a few words, but it had the same nasal lisp that I remembered.

"Hi, Auntie Virginia. I'm fine. In fact I raided your medicine chest and I'm flying all over the place." It was Terry.

"That's all you get. Bring the list to your usual drop off. I'll be there with the kid." There was an evil laugh and a hiccup. "If I feel like it."

"Wait! I have to go get the list. It's in a safe place but it will take me about half an hour to get it. Let me give you my cell phone number."

"I thought you didn't have a cell phone. Being an old lady and all. None of your customers said anything about a cell phone."

"It's borrowed. Just give me that much time. I'll have it for you."

"Don't keep me waiting. I get crazy when I wait." I heard the beep of his cell phone being disconnected.

"He really thinks I'm Virginia. The question is, what the hell was Ginny up to? And where the hell is 'the usual place?' And where does he have Terry?" Lucille hung up the phone just as my cell buzzed.

"Hi, this is Honey. Who in God's name is this?"

"Yeah, and a royal hello to you too. You know a guy with two bad feet? He's on crutches and has a rotten attitude. He flagged me in town wanting a ride to the Northampton airport. I took him a block down and shoved him out. No one calls me a dumb broad. Especially when he wanted the other dumb broad that drives for Cool Rides. Now, who would that be?"

"Hi, Belle."

"Plus, he critiqued my new nails. He called the color puke purple. And he told me to get a haircut. And then he pulled a big gun out of his crotch."

"Whoa, what'd you do?"

"I pulled out a bigger gun. That man is goin' down."

"He wanted a ride to the airport?"

"Well, he didn't get it from me."

Lucille and I said "airport" at the same time.

"Bye." I clicked off the phone over Belle's protests and Lucille and I headed out the door. Then we remembered that Jon had the keys to his car.

"Care to tell me what's going on and whether I need back-up or just duct tape?" Jon dangled the keys from one hand.

"Empty hangars. You can call for back-up on the way or maybe when we get there and decide if that's what Terry was telling us." We were already getting in the car. "And you have handcuffs, so you don't need duct tape."

Jon joined us and started the car.

"Northampton airport," I said.

Jon radioed in his destination. "I may need back-up. I'll appraise when I get there."

We pulled into the parking lot by Northampton Air's office. There was a black SUV parked to one side of the lot. A few white feathers still clung stubbornly to the license plate. Lucille got out of Jon's car, walked over to the SUV and shot out two of the tires.

"What the hell?" Jon bolted out of his car. He looked like he might grab Lucille's gun.

She smiled at him and said, "Prevention is always best."

Jon nodded and went into the office. Lucille and I followed, with Lucille looking quite satisfied with herself.

Jon pulled his badge out and showed it to the clerk. "We need to know who's come in and where the owner of the black SUV out front is."

"Huh." The clerk peered around the door to see the SUV with its newly flattened tires. "That's the guy who came in on that Citation parked out there by the end hangar. Hasn't even pulled the stairs yet. I think they have something in there. Some weird-looking guy met him. Had a kid with him, the weird guy. He looked like a gorilla. Short legs, long arms. The weird guy, not the guy that flew in. The guy that flew in is an old geezer." He looked at Lucille. "Sorry, ma'am. An elderly gentleman. There was another pretty strange fella that came with the gorilla guy. He was havin' some trouble. He had crutches."

Lucille had already turned and started out the door.

"Shit, either the boss has arrived, or they have another hostage," said Jon and raced after her, pulling out his cell phone as he went.

I followed more slowly. By the time I got to the hangar, Jon was flat against the outside wall next to the person-sized door built into the big airplane-sized door. Lucille was behind him. They both had guns out. The plane was around the side of the hangar. I decided to wander over and see if I could stab its tires with my little Swiss army knife. When I got to the plane, the pilot was still in his seat. He waved to me.

"Hey, where did your passenger go?" I asked when he leaned out the window.

He pointed to the side door to the hangar. It was slightly ajar, so I walked over to see who was inside. I nudged the door open and saw Sherman Wolenski standing next to a desk.

"Sherman?" I asked. His presence did not compute in my fuddled brain.

Sherman jerked around and looked really unhappy to see me. "Honey? The cab driver? What the fuck, did you ask this whole shit town to join us?" He turned to Gorilla Guy. I guessed Sherman wasn't a hostage. He grabbed my wrist and pulled me inside. I could see a body on the other side of the desk. It looked dead. Judging from the feet, I gathered Toes had become a liability. Or maybe overdid the booze and had a touch of alcohol-related coma.

Terry was sitting in a chair with Gorilla standing next to him. Gorilla's gun was out and loosely pointed in Terry's direction. I glanced over toward the front of the building to see if maybe Jon and Lucille had made it inside. The view was blocked by a pile of packing crates. That meant Jon couldn't see us either.

"We're outta here," said Sherman. He pulled me to the bottom of the three stairs and pushed me up into the plane. My resistance was discouraged by Sherman's very big gun.

Gorilla grabbed Terry and scrambled after us. Gorilla pulled the stairs and slammed the door. Sherman convinced the pilot to take off without checking in with the tower by putting a gun to his head. As we taxied to the runway, I saw Jon come barreling out of the hangar. Unlike television, a real man on foot is no match for an airplane in a hurry. We were airborne before Jon could get within fifty feet. I wasn't

196

sure why they hauled us along, but visions of flying out the door at 2000 feet danced through my head.

"This went to shit fast," commented Sherman.

I didn't have all the players straight in this scenario. "What exactly is 'this'?" I asked him.

"You, you and your stupid friends. My expansion plans were on target until your silly old lady friend got stubborn. She didn't see the advantage to a merger."

"Which old lady friend are we talking about? I'm a small-town taxi driver. Most of my friends are old. Old people are the only ones who don't drive in this country."

"Yeah, and stupid over there." He pointed to Gorilla. "He couldn't tell one old lady from another. He kept getting the wrong one. The local talent in this dumb-as-a- stump city is beyond belief. Virginia Percy was the local dealer. She had all the PCAs organized and the old idiots with too many pain meds and not enough money feeding her a fortune in oxy. She was selling for pennies on the dollar. Completely undercutting the market. She had no idea what she was doing. A friggin' gold mine. And we were going to put it all together. My connections to the south, her local people. We could franchise it. Spread the concept all over the East Coast. But no, she got greedy or chicken or something. Herman turned me onto the whole idea. My big brother was dumber than a troglodyte, but he had the right info to make it work. And then numb-nuts here kept getting the wrong old lady. They all look alike to him. In fact, you, quite frankly, are a drag on the whole plan," he said, turning toward Gorilla.

I didn't think it was a good time to point out that Gorilla wasn't exactly "local talent." He was pretty dumb. Sherman got that part of it right.

"So, about your brother?" I left the question hanging, hoping Sherman would satisfy my morbid curiosity.

"Oh, him." Sherman looked around the airplane. "He was the dumbest of all. And a mean fucker besides. Taking his meds away was the smartest thing I ever did. I should've done it years ago. But then he might not have given me this brilliant idea about all those meds."

The Gorilla had moved over behind the pilot to take over Sherman's job of urging him to keep flying and not head back to the airport. Sherman raised his gun and shot Gorilla, who staggered back against the pilot, knocking him into something very hard. I heard a clunk and the pilot slumped in his seat. Small plane, flying low, that works okay for everyone except the guy who gets shot. Big plane at high altitude, maybe not so smart.

Sherman stared at the pilot for a second too long. I grabbed the fire extinguisher by the door. Swinging it with every ounce of off-balance strength I had, I connected with Sherman's head and he sank to his knees. Another tap and he hit the deck hard. Of course, now we had no one to steer the plane and it was starting to fly a bit erratically.

"Anyone know how to fly a plane?" I asked, thinking it was a rhetorical question.

Terry jumped over to the pilot's chair, yanked him to the floor and slid into the vacated seat. He steadied the plane, reached for the communications with the tower and requested permission to land.

I breathed out carefully and stammered, "Where did you learn to fly?"

"Library. Remember, New York public? I can land any aircraft on the computer simulators. Well, I can land a simulator, anyway. They have flight, drive and sail programs in the library. I finished the 24 hours of LeMans when I was twelve. I did the Indy 500 the next year. How difficult can this be?"

Tell that to Michael Schumacher, I thought. I wasn't even sure what Mr. Schumacher raced so I kept quiet.

Terry steered the plane in a big circle, approached the runway and set it down like a feather. He taxied to the hangar and brought it to a graceful stop. I heaved open the door and dropped the steps. There was quite a light show happening next to the hanger with three cruisers, two ambulances and a fire truck with all lights flashing.

"Holy shit, I need input. What happened here? Who's the geezer they were talking about? And what happened to your hair?" Belle stood with her hands on her hips.

Jon had holstered his weapon when he saw me come out without a gun at my back.

Lucille looked for Terry.

I touched my hair. The hair band had come out sometime during the struggle with Sherman when he pushed me onto the plane. The wind had finished the job. I looked like I had a blow out in a wind tunnel. I deplaned, and Jon wrapped his arms around me.

Terry's head popped out of the airplane's door. Lucille gave him a thumbs up and motioned him down. "That landing is something you can tell your kids and grandkids about. Or just explain it to me when you're ready," she said.

"It was such a trip." Terry was almost dancing with excitement. "Soo much different than a simulator. I gotta get me one of those things." He pointed to the Citation as the uniform cops swarmed on.

"I didn't have time to duct tape anyone. Gorilla won't need it, I don't think. He may be beyond needing restraint. But Sherman? He should be shot or something before you bring him off."

"Sherman?" It was a chorus from Lucille, Jon and Belle. I realized they had no idea who was at the top of the corporate ladder in this enterprise.

I heard "Clear!" from the uniforms as the EMTs followed them into the plane.

"I gotta pulse! Bring the gurney. Bring a few." The EMTs started shoving bodies down the steps. Gorilla came first. Apparently, Sherman's aim wasn't so great, and the Ape was still breathing. The pilot might have a hell of a headache, but he walked off with some support. Sherman had an EMT on each side and a cop reading him his rights and cuffing him from behind.

As he stepped off the bottom of the short stairs, Lucille stepped forward. "What a fucking waste of a good-looking man," she muttered.

"No?" I whispered.

She balled up her fist and nailed Sherman in the nose, stepping aside to avoid the blood spatter.

Sherman's knees gave up the battle to stay upright and he sagged to the ground.

"Those fire extinguishers pack a punch," I commented as he was deposited in the back of a squad car.

"Way to go, Lucille!" said Belle.

"That's my Grandma," said Terry and did a little dance. "Or maybe my Great Aunt," he corrected and grinned.

Jon shook his head and headed back into the hangar. The forensics unit had arrived. The coroner's van rolled up. The uniforms had called both after finding Toes inside. Sherman had wreaked a lot of havoc in a short period of time. Now I had time to wonder about Virginia.

Like where she was and what had she done.

Chapter Fifteen

Jon went with the ambulance that transported Sherman. He sent one of the officers with the coroner's van and two to the hospital in the second ambulance to keep an eye on Gorilla Guy. He called in a photo and got a name for him. We now knew him as Wryzinski Chaluska. Gorilla was way easier. He had a long list of arrests and even a few convictions, mostly in New York.

Hey, Sherman, I could have told you he wasn't local talent.

Lucille and Terry slid into the back of Belle's taxi and we drove away.

"I'll make a new batch of cookies," said Lucille. Lucille made cookies to calm her nerves. She had Zen baking down to a science.

When we got to Lucille's house, Terry jumped out of the taxi almost before it stopped. He bounded to the door, still euphoric about having flown and landed a real airplane. Lucille was a few steps behind him and I was starting up the sidewalk when Terry pushed open the door.

"Wait," yelled Lucille, realizing an unlocked door was not good.

But it was too late. Virginia pulled Terry in, slammed the door and we heard the locks clicking closed.

"Damn, I forgot she had keys," said Lucille as she pulled hers out of her bag.

"Don't even think about coming in here! I'm armed and I will use it on him if you try to open that door." Virginia's voice came through the solid wooden entrance.

"What is it with old ladies and guns around here?" squawked Terry.

Lucille motioned me away from the door. "Stay here and distract her," she whispered and disappeared around the side of the house.

There was nothing I could do if Virginia came out armed with anything more than her old lady fist. I pulled out my cell phone and called Jon.

"She's at Lucille's house. She says she's armed, and she's got Terry hostage," I whispered into the phone and dropped it back into my pocket.

I pounded on the door, hoping it would mask the sound of Lucille sneaking in the back. There was no response, so I reached over and banged the door again.

"Shut up!" screamed Virginia and shot the door. It left a big hole in the door and the back-driver's side tire on the taxi deflated. I backed up and looked around for something to hit the door from farther away.

There weren't any baseballs or bats lying around but an adrenaline spike made me suddenly more sensitive to my surroundings—the blue sky, the puffy white clouds, a big rabbit hopping across the lawn. The rabbit paused to nibble clover, oblivious to the human drama inside. Hop, nibble, hop, nibble. If Lucille saw him, she would trim his tail.

Suddenly the door crashed open. Terry stumbled out, shoved forward by Virginia. Her gun pushed into his back as she steered him toward the cab. The rabbit sat up to observe this silly human behavior. Its ears twitched forward.

Lucille stepped out of the open door, weapon up and ready. The bunny saw the Lucille/weapon combination and took off like a rocket. Apparently, the local bunny population had a fast learning curve. The rest of the human population could be ignored, but Lucille with a gun was not a trivial matter.

Bugs Bunny shot forward and collided with Terry's leg. Terry instinctively jumped to avoid the flying rodent, stumbled and crawled away. The rabbit lashed out with its thunder thighs. Long red scratches appeared on Virginia's shin. It turned and sank its front teeth into her leg.

Virginia let out a screech of pain followed by, "Rabies, lock jaw, black plague!" She grabbed for the rabbit and dropped her gun which exploded and shot the other tire on my taxi.

Terry crab-skittered around, putting the taxi between him and any old ladies with guns. Lucille's weapon discharged with a bang. The rabbit shot down the street to a safer lawn.

Virginia grabbed her ear, blood spurting between her fingers. "You shot my ear," she yelped.

Lucille walked over, shoved her to the ground and put her foot on Virginia's back.

"Don't you move a goddamn inch," she said as sirens wailed and police cruisers rounded the corner.

Jon jumped out of his unmarked, weapon in hand and stopped when he saw Lucille with her foot on Virginia.

Chapter Sixteen

"Everyone is okay, I think," I said.

Jon shook his head, holstered his weapon and started laughing.

He got himself under control and strolled over to Lucille. He reached down and, like all cops know how, pulled Virginia up. She stood glaring at the ground. Her steel magnolia attitude had left her and she suddenly became five feet tall again.

Jon cuffed her, recited her Miranda rights and then looked over at Lucille.

"Yes, Virginia, there is a jail and it looks like you're going there," he said. "We've had a long and profitable talk with Sherman."

At a signal from Jon, one of the uniforms came over. Ginny was hauled off to cop central, hissing curses on Lucille. I didn't know exactly what she would be charged with. There were so many possibilities. Kidnapping Terry for a short period was only the first.

Terry was standing on the far side of my tilted cab. Two new tires were going to go over with Willie like a visit from the IRS. Maybe Jon could run interference for me.

Now that Ginny was safely gone, Terry came slowly out from behind the car. He looked around for any old ladies with guns, decided there were none that were dangerous, cast about for wayward rabbits and relaxed slightly. His look of vulnerability was so like a fifteen-year old that I almost forgot that he had just landed an airplane and assisted in the capture of some very bad people.

"Hi Terry," said Jon. "My name is Lieutenant Jon Stevens, with the Northampton Police Department. I don't think we've been formally introduced. You must be Lucille's grandnephew. And good luck with that." Jon smiled conspiratorially and shook Terry's reluctantly offered hand.

Lucille came over, stepped around Jon and stood beside Terry. The message was clear and Jon didn't miss it. Mama bear had come to the cub's defense.

Jon grinned at Lucille. "Start getting that I.D. taken care of. Make sure he's old enough to fly a plane. We'll talk later." It always surprised me how much Jon knew that I didn't know he knew.

He walked over to me. He brushed his lips over mine and said, "I'm glad to see your luck is holding. I will want those tires." He motioned the last uniform over to stay with the tires. He ran a finger down the side of my face, shook his head and got in the car.

I was pretty sure all the bad people were in police custody or dead, but I understood that Terry might not be sure who was a threat to him. Drug dealers were a known quantity in his world. Old ladies with guns and crazy taxi drivers weren't in his usual reality. And then there were the police. His experience painted them as the enemy. He would have a lot of adjustments to make. He wasn't even sure of his age. That could be a disadvantage under some circumstances. With Lucille in charge he would be able to pick his own birthday. I thought about what day I would pick if my choice was wide open. Probably spring, middle of the month, the sun would be shining, and all would be right with the world. Could that be arranged, please? My mother told me that I was born during a hurricane in the middle of the night and I refused to come out at all. She pushed for days. My father told me that was her version. Reality was very different.

Lucille herded Terry toward the house.

"We have some phone calls to make, young man. Applications up the wazoo to fill out," she said.

I had plenty of time to drive back to Cool Rides, but I had the little problem of two flat tires. I called in and explained the situation to Mona. Willie was on his way to Boston, thank God.

"You have what? How could you get two flats? Those tires were brand new. I might need to shoot someone."

"That's the problem. Someone shot the tires. Actually, it was Virginia Percy."

Silence on the other end of the line.

"And she had a gun, because?" asked Mona.

"Apparently she had some alternate sources of income. But right now, I need to get the tires fixed. Then we can talk."

"I'm sending Rigger."

Rigger arrived with two new wheels, tires already attached. He swapped them out for the bullet-riddled ones which he handed over to the officer. They went in the trunk of the patrol car and we were suddenly without any police presence. I heaved a sigh of relief and leaned against the car.

"Long day at the office?" asked Rigger.

"Exciting anyway. What's happening back at the garage?"

"You gotta come see Belle. She's coming in at 5:30 for a 6:00 pick up."

"So? Who's she driving?"

"Uh uh," grinned Rigger. "She's being driven. I'm picking her up at six and driving her to Mrs. Witherspoon's house in Florence Heights." He glanced at his watch. "Shit, we're calling it close. Gotta go if she's gonna be on time to her first family dinner with the judge and Mother Judge."

"She can't drive herself?"

"She refuses to leave her new Mini on the street in the Heights. So I'm delivering her to a meet-the-mother dinner."

"Whom she already knows."

"Yeah, but not like this. They're having dinner at Mom's house. It's like, hey, Mom, this is the one. The Judge is doing the cooking."

"And Belle agreed to go? What's she thinking?"

"She's thinking she's gonna seduce him tonight. She thinks that should scare the shit out of him. Or get him over the thrill of making it with a reformed prostitute or something. I can't figure out what she's thinking." Riggs shook his head.

"Neither can she. A confusing relationship is a new experience for her. She's never confused."

"Anyway, I'm getting back to taxi central before she backs out of this."

"Why's she meeting you at the garage? You could pick her up at home."

"Because she don't go nowhere without her fashion consultant giving her the all clear. And

208

between my last fare and your tire disaster, I didn't have time to get to her house. Gotta hustle," he said and hopped in his taxi.

I followed him down the street.

We arrived at Cool Rides just as Belle pulled up in her Mini. She opened the door and extended one long perfectly-shaped leg ending in three-inch heels on a conservative but beautifully made black leather shoe with a fine red line around the edge. She swung her matching leg and shoe to the ground. Her skirt came just above the knee. The ruffled edge was fluttered, draping gracefully over her thigh. It was also black with four red triangular gores adding fullness and color without bulk. Her blouse was cut low enough to make the judge notice and high enough not to offend his mother. An edge of black lace ran around the neckline. Her hair was shorter with a few ringlets framing her face. Her nails had been toned down to deep red.

"I feel sorry for Carlton the Judge," said Rigger.

"He doesn't stand a chance."

Mona came out of the office. She looked at Belle. "Oh, he is so cooked." She grinned.

Willie, back from his Boston run, wandered in from the garage, wiping his hands on a rag.

"Holy Mother. Where're you going?"

Mona turned to him. "Get with the program, William. She's settling her questions with the Judge tonight. She's having dinner with Mama."

"Mrs. Witherspoon? Give her my best. Wonderful lady," Willie said and fled back to the garage.

We were standing around, gawking at Belle when we heard the whoop of a siren. Jon's unmarked barreled around the corner and screeched to a stop. Jon jumped out.

Belle stiffened slightly.

"Hey, Jon," I said. "How goes the battle?"

"Not well. Virginia Percy has escaped. You need to be careful. She probably won't go after Belle. Honey and Lucille are more likely targets. Personally, I'm hoping she's halfway to Mexico or Canada. Or at least across the Massachusetts state line. Add to that a five car pile-up on the interstate. It's been a war zone."

I stood speechless. How does an eighty-something year old lady escape?

"Honey, you need to spend the night at my house."

I scowled at Jon.

"Okay, Honey, for your own safety, would you be willing to stay at my house tonight?"

"You bet," I said. Jon was learning not to push my buttons too much. "So how are you going to cover Lucille? Can she and Terry stay in your house? And how did Virginia escape? She's an eighty-year old little old lady. What happened?" The tenser I got, the more I babbled.

"The guard made the same mistake about age. Virginia Percy asked the guard to take her to the, I quote, 'young ladies' room' where Virginia flushed a roll of toilet paper. The guard went in to unplug it and Virginia Percy pushed the woman's head into the toilet until she passed out. Miss Virginia Percy, the southern gentlewoman, stripped the guard, put on the uniform and I.D., took her gun and walked out the front door. The guard is lucky to be alive."

"Never underestimate the elderly," I said. "How are they doing with Sherman?"

"More carefully. The gun that he had on the plane was used in a homicide in New York City a year ago. Sherman Wolenski is going down for first degree murder."

"Holy shit, never underestimate the elderly," I repeated softly.

Lucille had trained Jon well enough that he wouldn't make that kind of mistake. When you live next door to a female geezer who can out-shoot you on the target range, you tend to be realistic about aging.

"How are you going to protect Lucille, if she needs it?"

"I have an officer staying in her house until we find our escapee."

"Uh oh. How did she react to that?"

"I got Rodriguez to do the duty. Lucille told me she could watch, and again I quote, 'that hunk of man flesh' all day. He promised to bring some of his hand drums along and give Terry some drumming lessons."

"Is he sure Terry hasn't already mastered that in the New York Library system? I bet he's had a few music lessons."

Jon sighed. "Whatever," he said.

Rigger and Belle were about to get in the Cool Rides taxi when Rigger's private cell rang. He stepped away from the group to take the call.

When he returned, the expression on his face was apologetic. "That was Henry. He just came off dealing with your five-car pileup from the interstate and doesn't think he's in condition to drive. He was hoping I could come get him."

"Hey, I can drop Belle off at Florence Heights and go right to Jon's house. I have an airport in the morning so I'm taking a car home."

"Thanks," said Rigger.

Belle nodded. "Go give him the support he needs. Honey and I are on our way."

Jon looked a little worried that he had to let me go anywhere.

"Virginia Percy is probably halfway to wherever she wants to escape to by now. I'll just drop Belle off and be at your house in less than a half hour. Go home and check on Lucille. She's a more likely target anyhow."

"I'll see you in half an hour. No more."

We all split up, Jon to his house, Rigger to the hospital and Belle and me to Mrs. Witherspoon's house.

I sincerely hoped that the elderly escapee had headed for the border.

Chapter Seventeen

"So, what's the plan?" I asked Belle the minute we were in the car and on our way.

"What plan? I'm having dinner with some nice people. That's the plan."

"Bull cocky. You're going to scare the daylights out of Judge Carlton Witherspoon. What are you gonna do? Offend his mother? Tell her that her son should get real about being involved with you? Belle, this guy is the best thing that ever happened to you and you shouldn't mess it up."

"Honey, I'm just going for dinner. I'm going to keep it simple and open. I like Mrs. W. I would never offend her. I enjoy giving her rides downtown. But this is her son bringing home a friend. It's a different dynamic. And I don't think anything scares Carlton. He's been in some very weird situations."

"Yeah? Care to share?"

"Too late," said Belle as we turned into Florence Heights. I pulled up a few doors from Mrs. Witherspoon's apartment. There was the usual assortment of cars in various states of decomposition, dismembered toys, bicycles and a few dead plants. A dumpster was rusting and overflowing farther down the block and I thought about Rigger and the dumpster diving skunks. Mrs. W's house stood out like a well-manicured thumb amid the chaos of debris.

213

I parked and, in keeping with the spirit of the occasion, I got out, opened the door for Belle and escorted her up the sidewalk. I knocked and was opening the door when I felt the pressure of a cold round piece of steel against my backbone.

"Just go right in," said Miss Virginia Percy and shoved us through the door.

I stumbled slightly and looked up to see Mrs. Witherspoon standing by the living room couch. She was about to deposit a plate of bacon-wrapped somethings on the coffee table. Carlton was coming in from the kitchen. We all froze while Virginia assessed the situation. Mrs. W put the plate down on one of the end tables, next to the Waterford crystal candlestick. There was a matching one on the other end table. Probably the real deal. Possibly a gift from the Judge. The décor was an interesting mixture of pre- "my son has a good job" Goodwill and post- "he's finally through law school" expensive gifts.

But Virginia wasn't there to admire the home furnishings.

She moved over so we were all within her range of vision. She was still wearing the prison guard uniform. It was too big and she had cinched it tighter around her waist with the standard issue belt. It still bagged around her shoulders and the legs dragged a little on the ground. She looked like someone had tied a brown tent around her body. I reminded myself that it fit well enough to let her walk out of the jail without anyone challenging her.

"I was just visiting one of my many friends in the Heights when who should I spot pulling up? A taxi and driver. Just what I happen to need at the moment. I could use some food as well. I haven't eaten since my unfortunate incident at the hands of this idiot here." She waved the gun in my direction with one hand and snatched a bacon-wrapped thingy off the plate with the other.

"What can we do for you, my dear?" asked Mrs. Witherspoon. I realized she didn't know Virginia Percy.

"This bag of southern white cracker scum is an escaped prisoner and drug dealer," said Belle.

Virginia turned to Belle. "Watch your mouth, you piece of black pussy. I have a full clip of bullets in this gun." She popped the food into her mouth and turned the gun toward Belle.

Belle and I edged away from the Judge and Mrs. W, widening the area Virginia had to keep track of.

"Don't move any more. I like to shoot guns. Lucille helped me develop a taste for that."

The Judge, ignoring Virginia's request, moved between his mother and the weapon. Virginia swung it in his direction. The gun went off with a bang, winged the Judge in the thigh and exploded the crystal candlestick on the end table.

"Damn, must be a hair trigger," muttered Virginia.

The Judge went down like an airplane with no landing gear. Belle jumped over to him, tore off her jacket and pressed it against the Judge's thigh, which was bleeding a lot. It wasn't spurting so at least the bullet didn't hit an artery.

"Honey!" Belle yelled. "Get over here and lean on this while I tie a tourniquet." She ripped off the arm of her blouse and started to tie it around the upper leg.

215

"Don't move any fucking farther or I will try out this very sensitive trigger again," snarled Virginia.

I knelt next to Belle and applied pressure to the wound.

The Judge raised his head and groaned.

Belle stood up and took a step toward Virginia. "You little snot. You look older than the wood on Noah's fucking ark. And you just shot an officer of the court. Even worse, you just shot a friend of mine."

"And you look like you should be giving back alley blow jobs in the Calcutta slums. Is that a fashion statement or a porn star costume? We should never have let you people come over from Africa."

"Your southern hemline is showing, you hunk of wheezing overripe rotten fried tomato."

Belle inched closer.

Virginia pointed the gun.

No one seemed to notice that the other elder in the room had moved into Virginia's blind spot.

The Judge's mother picked up the matching Waterford candlestick, raised it over her head and swung down with the force of an angry mother bear. The beautiful candlestick exploded. Virginia sank to her knees and face planted onto the Oriental rug.

"Well, it wouldn't make sense to have just one." Mrs. Witherspoon held the shattered glass base. Belle grabbed some duct tape out of her bag.

But Mrs. Witherspoon beat her to it. She grabbed a roll of paisley pink duct tape out of the kitchen junk drawer. If she and Lucille ever got their junk drawers combined, they could conquer the known universe.

I pulled my phone out and dialed 911.

"We need an ambulance," I said and gave her the address. Then I punched in Jon's number on my speed dial. Time to face the disbelief on his face when he arrived.

"Stevens. Where are you?" Jon's voice had a touch of panic in it. I heard a siren in the background.

"I'm at Mrs. Witherspoon's house. The situation is under control." *Be professional*, I said to myself. Well, try, anyhow.

"Does this involve duct tape?"

"Yes, but it's not mine. And it's paisley. I didn't know you could get it in paisley," I said. *The adrenaline must be wearing off*, I thought. Again.

"I'm right around the corner and there's an ambulance behind me. Who's hurt?"

"The Judge. But we stopped the bleeding."

"Jesus! What happened? Never mind. I'm coming in." The phone went dead.

"Bye, Jon. Hi, Jon," I said as he rushed through the door.

Virginia was starting to move when the EMTs barreled in.

"That the patient?" asked the first one.

"Maybe take that one first," I pointed to the Judge as Belle yelled, "Over here!"

They hauled the Judge out on a stretcher with Belle and Mrs. W in tow. Everyone loaded into the ambulance and they took off, full siren. One EMT stayed behind to deal with Miss Virginia Percy, escapee and possible killer. For her, they called a special ambulance. The EMT thought she had a concussion, but nothing dangerous even for her age.

217

"I think I'll call in a guard and let's cuff her to the roll around."

The second ambulance arrived five minutes after the first had left. They strapped Virginia down and cuffed her to the metal side bars.

I walked out with Jon to watch them load her up. Strapped and cuffed, her arms were immobilized. Her legs dangled loosely over the end. They rolled the gurney onto the street, up the rise in the pavement and lined it up with the open door of the ambulance. Her left foot twitched as she regained awareness. Suddenly both legs flew straight up, lashed out and caught the EMT square in the jaw. He staggered back, losing his grip on the gurney. It drifted slowly down the incline, away from the ambulance.

Jon ran after it and dived for the stretcher. He hoisted himself to his knees on top of Miss Virginia. Unfortunately, this added weight and momentum. Also unfortunately, there was no steering mechanism on the moving bed. They zipped gracefully down the street, Jon beating back Virginia's knees, which she kept aiming for his crotch. They crash-landed into the side of a dumpster. Jon did a flying dismount, the gurney upended, and a screeching Miss V flattened against the dumpster, creating a gurney, Virginia, dumpster sandwich.

There was silence except for Jon's heavy breathing, the pounding of the EMT's shoes on pavement and the scratching of one wheel of the gurney against the dumpster. Then there was a smell distinctively different from the dumpster odor. I saw a black-and-white tail disappear under the rusted edge of metal as Jon back-pedaled away from the disaster.

We all stood for a few minutes staring at the scene, mostly wanting to not touch anything. Finally one of the EMTs handed out little paper masks to everyone. We all slipped them over our mouths and the EMT approached the gurney.

"I got a pulse, I think," the EMT called out when he leaned into the middle of the sandwich and felt Miss V's neck.

Jon and the EMT pried the gurney and Miss V off the dumpster and rolled her back up to the waiting transportation. Her nose was a little flatter and she had some bright red scrapes on her cheeks. Both knees were skinned, and blood was leaking through that area of the prison uniform. The EMT and Jon managed to straighten her legs and strap them down. She was looking like a ball of oversized string, but she wasn't going to get away again on Jon's watch.

They were about to push her through the open doors into the ambulance cave when her eyes popped open. She tried to spit at Jon but her mouth was too dry. "Give me a fucking drink," she hissed.

"You are so under arrest. You have the right to remain silent but, just so you know, Sherman and his sidekick are singing like demented roosters," said Jon as he tightened the leg straps.

She was turning a bright shade of purple as they heaved her inside.

Jon turned to me.

I backed up. He had been closer to the drifting skunk than I had.

"I'm going with her to the hospital. I'll meet you at my house and pick up my car later." He paused at the door of the ambulance. "Honey, go straight to my house. Go to Lucille's side and STAY there until I finish up with this disaster."

"Try to get a shower and put on some of those scrubs things at the hospital, like before you come home," I yelled from a distance and saluted him, holding my keys aloft so he could see that I was headed for the taxi.

The ambulance pulled away without sirens and headed toward the hospital. Our steel magnolia had turned into the wicked witch. Belle had made the ultimate impression on Carlton's mother. And I was left standing alone with my taxi in Florence Heights. What could go wrong?

I was walking over to the taxi when I heard screaming. It came from across the street. That wasn't too unusual in the Heights, so I didn't pay much attention.

A door slammed, and a big guy stormed out. "I need a ride," he yelled at me.

"Ok, I'm going downtown. I can give you a lift."

The door slammed again, and a large woman stood on the top step. She screeched and charged down the stairs. "You fucker! Don't you ever call my mama an old farting battle-axe again. And don't expect to spend any more nights here!" She brandished a gun over her head.

"Oh, stuff a sock in it, you old pig. You couldn't hit the Goodyear blimp with that thing if it was sitting on your doorstep."

"Oh yeah?"

"Yeah!"

She lowered the gun and pointed it in our direction. I jumped one way and the big guy jumped the other. I scurried behind an ancient half-stripped car a few spaces away.

She fired off a round and the taxi window shattered into a zillion pieces of glittering glass.

"Shit! Hold still and I'll show you who can hit that limp blimp that hangs between your legs!" She raised the gun again. There was a bang and my front tire sank to the pavement.

I cowered behind the rusted car.

"Okay, now I got no transpo. How the hell am I supposed to leave? That's what you wanted, isn't it?" He sniffed the air. "Hey, maybe that wasn't your mother's fart."

"Maybe, maybe not. Where you gonna go? I mean what you want me to do? You can't say that kind of stuff."

"Yeah, okay, so I might've been a bad mouth about your momma. Let me back in and maybe we can make it up, okay?"

"Whatever." And the big lady sashayed back inside.

The guy followed her.

I walked over to my taxi. I sighed. I went around to the hatchback and pulled out the spare tire and jack. Maybe if I changed the tire and made it back to the garage, Mona wouldn't get too hissy about the window. As if. And then there was Jon. I would need Mona to give me another taxi for the morning run and keep Jon in a good mood so I could turn into a zombie in front of his big screen TV.

I was running out of time and energy and changing a flat would consume both. I was so tired, I actually considered making the screaming couple's life more miserable by reporting the gun shot and damage to the car. I had the spare tire out and stood staring morosely at the deflated one when the big guy in question came out.

"Need a hand?" he asked. He sniffed the air. "I guess Sweet Petunia nailed someone, huh? I figured it was the old lady's old lady."

"Need a strong back and some extra energy," I said crossly. "Who's Sweet Petunia?"

"Lemme help you out, little lady." He flexed his bicep and stepped closer to the car. "Sweet P is the resident skunk. Smells like she missed you and your car."

I was torn between using the tire iron on his bald head and just letting it all go and watching him sweat instead of me. I chose the latter.

When I finally got back to the garage, Mona was more sympathetic than I expected. She heard what happened because Rigger and Belle had crossed paths at the hospital. I had to explain the flat tire and shattered window, but she muttered about insurance and offered to give me a ride to Jon's house.

"I'll take it," I said and got there before Jon.

It took a long time to process all the witness statements and he would be doing more of that tomorrow when I went in for a formal sit down.

When he finally got back, Jon went next door to Lucille's unit. He sent Rodriguez home but not before Rodriguez left Terry with a small hand drum which Lucille finally pried out of his hands at eleven that night.

When Jon came back to his side of the house, I was nodding off on the couch as whatever show I was watching was winding down. He leaned over to kiss my hair and nuzzle my neck. I sniffed, and then I sniffed again. "You have a slight but very distinct odor. You may need another shower or two or three. I've heard that tomato juice helps get rid of that special smell."

He grinned at me. "I already checked it out on the Internet. Hydrogen peroxide, baking soda and lots of slippery dish soap. I might need help to get it slathered all over me." He paused. "And all over you."

"I'll get the soap," I said.

An hour later Jon lay on the bed, smelling like a clean dish.

"I never knew that dish soap could be so…" I was searching for a word.

"Slippery," said Jon.

Slippery didn't begin to describe it.

I had a smile that I couldn't get under control and I was silently thanking God, again, that Jon had already found the map to the female orgasm. And he didn't need a GPS.

Chapter Eighteen

When all the witnesses were interviewed, all the accused were charged with various crimes, played against each other, plea-bargained according to how bad the crimes were and how good the information was. The cops had busted a major prescription drug ring and prevented the new one from coming into town.

In interviewing Virginia Percy, everyone kept their distance. She still smelled pretty bad. Jon had donned hospital duds and trashed his clothes. The EMTs had stripped the ambulance of anything that absorbed smell and dumped it all in the medical waste bin.

But no one except Virginia Percy needed any pain meds. And she was given them sparingly. No outside visitors who might walk out with any extra pills were allowed.

This didn't mean there wouldn't be a new distribution of drugs in short order. There would always be someone ready to step into the void. My fare that died in the crossfire turned out to only be the opening salvo in the local turf war. It was Sherman's first attempt to hire local talent and Virginia's first defense of her territory. A corporate takeover and that poor shmoe had just gotten caught in the middle. And now he was dead. That meant little Miss Ginny was guilty of first-degree murder. Toes had died of alcohol poisoning and Fingers seemed to be recovering so Sherman would only have a dozen or so other charges to face, but not murder, in this state, anyway. New York might have a few requests of their own.

But for now at least, Northampton was no longer the hub of the prescription drug trade. Now the goods would have to be imported from farther down the interstate.

Sherman and Virginia were trying to outdo each other in the squeal department, singing like canaries looking for a way out of the coal mine. They could have cooperated, both become rich and made Northampton a poorer place. Thank God they got greedy.

Virginia had organized a combination of seniors who needed money more than pain killers and personal care attendants who had excessive access to people in pain who had excessive access to pain-killing drugs. She didn't sell anything in her own backyard. She bought local and sold to a wholesaler down the interstate who probably sent some of it back up into Virginia's backyard.

Sherman learned about all this from his big brother, Herman Wolenski, who had used Virginia's services more than once. Where Virginia saw a nice income, Sherman saw a gold mine. He was ready to import talent to sell local and continue the flow to the south. He had contacts in New York City and they had contacts with kids like Terry. Terry's job would have been to control the distribution to the local teen market. But they misjudged Terry's outlook on life. He liked people and that made it impossible for him to add the misery of drug addiction to their lives. He didn't have much information about the operation because he jumped ship early on. But he did know some of the New York contacts, and that would put more leverage in the hands of the police.

Lucille and I talked that night after Virginia was arrested the first time.

"I really messed up on Virginia. I should know better than to assume some of the stuff I did. I thought she was living on Social Security and a pension. I should have noticed that she had more money than that. Her occasional forgetfulness, her complaints about chronic pain, I guess mostly a very clever act."

Lucille herself was a living contradiction to some of those assumptions. We both assumed that all the seniors who complained about losing their pain meds were just forgetful.

"Even seniors generalize about other seniors, I guess," I said, trying to be sympathetic.

"Not all people over sixty are forgetful. Not all of them are in pain. And not all of them are poor or rich. Most of us are just like everyone else. In the middle and trying to survive. The difference with the elderly is that we are frequently marginalized and ignored. We get stuck in retirement homes. We're well cared for but, essentially, warehoused until we drop dead."

I thought about how much I had learned just listening to Lucille. What could the elderly tell us about avoiding conflict? They lived through some of the worst times in human history. They should be writing the history books filled with real history, no holds barred, no white-washed facts. Of course, God only knows what history according to Lucille would be like.

Lucille sighed. "When we're young, we scramble to make ends meet. It's a challenge and kind of fun. When you get older, you see the inequities of the whole system and the scramble isn't so fun anymore. Sometimes it's almost impossible. Maybe Ginny just wanted to stop scrambling," she said.

I wasn't so sure I agreed with that assessment of Ginny. "Ginny showed a nasty side when she got cornered, you know. She was not a nice person," I replied.

But I did understand what she was saying about the scramble. I enjoy the challenge. I've never been rich, so I don't know if that would make a difference in my behavior or my enjoyment of life. I hope I will grow old as gracefully and with as much chutzpa as Lucille.

Virginia Percy claimed that the drug dealing gig was her way of helping out the elder population when they couldn't make ends meet. That didn't explain her willingness to shoot someone in the back to protect her operations. What made someone able to kill like that? Both Virginia and Sherman seemed quite able to pull a lethal trigger to protect their turf. I thought about the strange and weird people I knew and the ones I met driving a taxi. Were any of them capable of shooting to kill? Mona had talked about getting guns for all her drivers to carry. That might be okay for Belle and any of the other drivers. My aim is so bad I would be just as likely to shoot my foot as to bring down a serial killer.

Belle was looking at long-term relationships a little differently. She'd learned a lot when the judge lay bleeding on the floor. Maybe the Judge might convince her to have honorable intentions. Circumstances being what they were, she hadn't seduced him...yet. But she ruined a sexy shirt for a tourniquet on his leg, so that needed replacing and that meant a shopping spree. I could pick up another pair of shoes, or as Belle called them, FMS. To quote Belle; "There is nothing like the weight of a good man between a good woman's legs. And 'fuck me shoes' can make that happen."

But tonight Lucille had invited the whole taxi company and friends over for a real dinner party.

When Judge Carlton heard that the gentlemen would be watching the game on Jon's big screen TV, he said he wouldn't miss dinner with Miss Lucille for the world. The ladies would watch football on Lucille's big screen TV. That way the guys didn't have to listen to girly comments, mostly from Lucille about why the quarterback had a towel hanging over his package. She considered said package to be so well contained as to be meaningless to the females in the crowd. So she focused on butts and tats. The men were free to discuss defense and offense and general strategy.

Carlton had laid down a few rules. The cases against Virginia Percy, in which he might be a victim, and against Sherman Wolenski, in which he might be a judge, were off limits for dinner table discussion. We had plenty of other topics to cover. Carlton arrived sporting a cane. His limp was gone but he liked the cane.

Terry's new birthday and identification was a hot topic. He had chosen October first for his birthday, his reasoning being that the closest holiday was Halloween. That way he wouldn't miss out on the greed train and not get enough gifts. Fifteen was his chosen official age. No one knew his real age, but at fifteen he could go back to his senior year among his peers in high school or he could take the high school equivalency exam and go straight to community college where he would get courses designed to advance a career as a pilot. He would also be learning to fly a real airplane and get his pilot's license at the local airport. Not that he didn't already know how, but, in this situation, the piece of paper was important.

Lucille was looking into adoption. She didn't have children. Her husband had passed over a year ago, so she was looking for a family connection. Jon was as close to family as she had. There were advantages to adopting a teenager. No diapers to change. Still, lots of teenage angst.

"Life is always a trade-off," said Lucille when we talked about Terry.

When we arrived, Lucille had set a formal table with place cards and real cloth napkins. Jon sat next to Belle which promised some lively conversation. Willie was next to Mrs. Witherspoon which put him at ease. Mona and Terry were side by side. Maybe it was an attempt to integrate Terry into the local social scene since Mona knew everyone in the city. I sat next to Henry, who was now officially engaged to Rigger, who was at the head of the table opposite Lucille in the other power seat. We were eating off Lucille's best china plates. All the food was on the passthrough from the kitchen so Lucille could grab and pass. Boarding house reach was encouraged. We settled in and Mrs. Witherspoon insisted on a short thanks-be-to-God that we were all here. We probably each worshiped or didn't worship different Gods.

Everyone glanced around, and Belle raised her glass. We all joined her.

"Here's to working women everywhere." She looked over at Carlton. "And working men, no matter how they earn a living."

"It's good to have a work ethic," said Lucille. She grabbed the main dish and passed it to her left.

"Whoa, this is fabulous," said Belle after we served ourselves and dug in.

"Very tasty," said Mrs. Witherspoon.

"Hey, I like this," echoed Terry.

They were right. It was excellent.

"So, what is this?" I asked cautiously.

Lucille smiled beatifically. "Rabbit stew." Her gaze traveled around the table and noted our looks of horror. The rabbit had saved us from attempted kidnapping by Virginia, after all.

"But it's vegetarian," she added quickly.

Epilogue:

Vegetarian rabbit stew recipe:

Ingredients:

Whatever the rabbits leave in the garden.

Toss all the ingredients in a pot and boil until done. Suggested option—toss a chicken in there with them. It's still vegetarian if you're a rabbit, not so much if you're a chicken.

The rabbits had staged a midnight raid on Lucille's garden. She had carrots, potatoes, beans, peas, tomatoes and squash left. The rabbits had stomachs full of broccoli, cabbage, carrot tops and lettuce.

Read on for an excerpt
from Honey Walker's next adventure:

Taxi Scramble

by

Harriet Rogers

Chapter One

Fascination and terror short circuited my brain as the skinny guy in line ahead of me shoved a gun in the clerk's face and demanded money. It was one of those "I can't look away" moments.

The convenience store clerk shrugged and held out a wad of singles, as if this were an everyday occurrence.

The robber snatched the bills, grabbed an open carton of jumbo Snickers off the display, shot the ceiling, and bolted out the door. Ceiling pieces rained down as I watched the hold-up guy through the glass wall that covered the front of the building.

High-speed disaster turned to a slow-mo "Oh God, please don't" moment when I saw the passenger side door of my taxi open. Lucille, my elderly passenger, put one sensibly clad foot on the ground. The other foot followed, and she stomped forward. A snub-nosed pistol somehow moved from her bra holster to her hand. My mouth opened and squeaked a protest.

Lucille is possibly, maybe, could be, somewhere in age between seventy and infinity, with a background that included knowing a lot about weaponry. We had stopped at the convenience store to pick up milk to go with cookies she had baked to curry favor with taxi drivers, friends, relatives and, most of all, the male population at the local Senior Center.

I hammered on the automatic door until it reluctantly reopened. By the time I got outside the would-be robber was stomach down, hands restrained behind his back with a pair of fuzzy purple cuffs. Lucille's gun was pointed at the ground, her sensibly clad foot holding the hoodie covered neck tightly against the pavement.

"Move one muscle and I will staple your junk to your ears and kneecap you," Lucille said sweetly.

I sighed, pulled out my cell phone and speed-dialed my personal police officer, Lieutenant Jon Stevens.

"Where are you and what have you done?" Jon asked.

"At the Stop and Go convenience store and I didn't do anything, but Lucille has a present for you and it's wearing purple handcuffs."

"Christ," Jon mumbled, and the phone went dead.

My name is Honey Walker and I drive a cab for Cool Rides Taxi in Northampton, Massachusetts. At five-six with curly blond hair, blue eyes and a button nose, I'm considered cute, sort of what people thought Shirley Temple should have looked like all grown up. Women usually like to hear words like striking, beautiful, gorgeous, even interesting. My best friend, Belle, would be all of those with an explosive side of glitter. But I'll settle for cute.

Northampton is a small town with a near schizophrenic mix of liberal and conservative small-town values. The excitement level has increased as the larger cities to the south export their criminal elements northward up the interstate. Although convenience stores have a high robbery rate, this was the first time I had witnessed one. I'm young and foolish enough to find it more interesting than terrifying.

Lucille rolled the over idiot who flunked Robbery 101 as I picked bits of ceiling tile out of my hair.

She gently pushed the dirty hood away from his face. "Why, you're just a child," she said. "I do hope I didn't frighten you with all that talk of staples and kneecapping."

A boy, not more than fifteen and possibly as young as twelve, stared up at us with panic and defiance.

"Unfortunately, we have already called the constabulary," Lucille said.

"Yeah, and I called the cops," said the clerk, joining us in the parking lot.

"So, how much did he get?" One of the customers had wandered over from the gas pump.

"Ten dollars cash and thirty-five dollars and sixty cents in Snickers, including tax," said the clerk. The gathering crowd looked at the rest of the candy bars scattered around our feet.

"Hey, once it hits the ground, I can't restock it. Help yourselves," he said, snatching one, tearing off the wrapper and downing the oversized bar in two bites. The word "evidence" ran briefly through my brain. The clerk picked up the wad of dollar bills that the thief had dropped in an oily puddle.

"I think I'll pop these in the microwave," he said.

Okay, no more microwave hotdogs for lunch from this place.

A crowd of patrons and passers-by stood around discussing the young robber's fate, the frequency of such incidents and the gourmet value of a Snickers bar.

A middle age woman in sweats squinted at the miniscule calorie label on the candy-bar. "Look at what's in this. How can two ounces of anything add five pounds of flab to my butt?"

"They should tell you more about the levels of bliss attained and less about calorie count." A younger woman swallowed at least a million calories.

"Perhaps bliss is not quantifiable," someone added.

"The positive outlook achieved by sweetening one's palate prolongs life."

"They say that each cigarette you smoke takes nine minutes off your life. Maybe eating a candy bar adds it back."

"Who needs to know how short their life is going to be?"

"I prefer Milky Way myself," said an elderly gentleman, plucking two Snickers out of a puddle.

"No way," said a passing teenager. "There's peanuts in that Snickers. The government says that a helping of nuts every day keeps you stronger longer."

"Do you believe everything the government tells you?" asked the old guy.

"Do you believe *anything* the government tells you?" asked a spandex-ed jogger.

"I got some hazelnut coffee inside. That gives you double the nuts so coffee and Snickers should keep you alive forever according to the government food pyramid," added the clerk.

The philosophic discussion of Snickers continued until the candy disappeared and sirens screamed up the street. A patrol car slid into the parking lot, spraying loose gravel, but the officers had missed dessert. Lucille continued to keep a close eye on the subdued robber until she handed him over to one of the uniforms.

Jon arrived shortly after the blue and white patrol car had screeched to a stop. Officers were interviewing witnesses. The kid was in the back of the cruiser with less colorful restraints. Purple handcuffs caused consternation among the uniforms, but Lucille smiled in her Debbie Reynolds' way and returned them to her over-sized shoulder-bag.

"So, why did you come?" I asked Jon, knowing a lieutenant wouldn't normally bother with such a mundane event.

"Entertainment."

Jon and I met a few years ago when he busted me for vagrancy and assaulting an officer, although the charges were dropped. We watched each other around town for a few years. Eventually we became close personal friends, then very close. The closer we got, the more he tried to assert authority over how I lived my life. He still tries to do the authority thing and I still ignore his efforts, but we get along where it counts. Spending a night with Jon usually involves good conversation, lots of fun, and more than one miracle moment. He is also Lucille's landlord in the Victorian two-family that he owns. She and her adopted son, Terry, are the "two" in the two-family house.

"What's going to happen to that boy?" asked Lucille, glancing at the back of the cruiser.

"I'll need to see if he's in the system first," said Jon. "Find out how old he is, if he has parents, guardian or foster care."

"There are a few things you will find out shortly about him." Lucille gazed at the patrol car.

"And what would that be?" asked Jon.

"When I applied the hand-cuffs I noticed cigarette burns on his arms and a crude tattoo, possibly a gang tag."

"I'll check it out." Jon watched the patrol car pull onto the street. "Nice handcuffs."

"Well, they aren't yours," replied Lucille.

"No, but most of the force knows where you live."

Lucille did the Mona Lisa smile.

We watched the departing cruiser as the crowd dispersed. The kid would be formally arrested and held at the Northampton jail until his case got sorted out.

I started back to retrieve the gallon of milk I had abandoned when the robbery broke out.

"Honey?" Jon called to me.

"What?"

"I'm glad you're okay." He smiled, strolled over to me and traced a finger down my neck. "Come over tonight," he added.

"Maybe. I have to bring Lucille home at the end of my shift. Do I get the remote?" I needed a football fix and Jon had a humongo flat screen TV. The mini TV in my apartment did no justice to the buns and tats of an NFL player.

"I'll be home around six." Jon kissed my nose. "Don't entertain me any more until tonight." He paused, added, "Please," ambled to his unmarked and drove off.

I went inside, collected my milk, looking at the slightly singed edges of the dollar bill the clerk gave me in change.

In the taxi, Lucille gripped her oversized, overstuffed purse. She had that spacey expression she gets when she is working out a particularly vexing problem.

I met Lucille several years ago when I drove her to the airport. She was transporting her husband's ashes to be scattered in some mysterious place that I didn't want to know about. Most of him got on the plane with Lucille. A few ashes leaked through a hole in his box to be sucked up by the airport vacuum and, possibly, into the nose of a drug sniffing beagle.

Right now, I dropped Lucille, her milk, cookies, quick release handcuffs and her roving eye at the Senior Center and drove back to the Cool Rides garage.

My best friend and fellow cabbie, Belle, was sitting outside in a plastic lawn chair watching the world go by. Her head was bobbing to music from headphones forced down over her four-inch Afro. I dragged out another chair and joined her six-feet of chocolate-brown womanhood.

"Where's Mona?" Mona, our dispatcher and general guardian of the cars, frequently joined Belle in people watching and the sport of fashion terrorism.

"Inside Zening over driver applications. She is one with her computer."

"Zening?" I was pretty sure Mona didn't practice any special religion, so I wasn't sure what Belle meant other than that we always needed drivers and Mona had computer programs that made the standard police check on potential drivers a waste of time. I leaned back and enjoyed the sun.

Belle smiled. "I believe the Urban Dictionary defines it as 'to be one with the world around you. While in this state of being everything works out for you and enjoyable things spontaneously show up.' She wants a really good new driver. 'Course you and me, we're a hard act to follow. How's Lucille?" Belle asked without shifting her eyes from a particularly muscular example of manhood jogging by in bright blue short-shorts and a banana yellow tank top.

"I dropped her at the Senior Center with enough cookies to snare any guy over 75 who knows what a vibrator is for."

"Umm, a woman with attitude, our Lucille."

"We had an incident when we stopped for milk to go with the cookies, but Lucille took care of it." I related the excitement and Jon's comments on my entertainment value.

"You better show him what real entertainment is about tonight." Belle stretched, wiggled her two-inch, two-toned fingernails, red and black today, with silver sparkle. I knew she had a pair of three-inch spike heels that matched the fingernails. They were probably stashed in her oversized shoulder-bag in case she had a date night with Judge Carlton Witherspoon. Carlton was slowly working past her defenses, mostly about her previous employment. She had been a very successful lady of the evening before her pimp was found with a bullet hole decorating the space between his eyes. She decided to change careers and taxi driving required a different set of people skills but a similar personality. She stretched again and sighed.

She fluffed up her Afro. "How's Terry?"

"He's gained weight so he's not a scarecrow anymore. For all his talk about eating like a king out of the dumpsters of New York, he was still young and scrawny when he came up here. Right now, he's thinking about the who, what, where and why of his existence."

"The *what* would be Lucille's cookies, the *where* is wherever she puts him, the *why* he's gonna have to figure out for himself. Life can't get more profound than that," said Belle, closing her eyes to the sun. "And he was scrawny because he spent much time running from the law and a lot of other people."

"The adoption papers came through. He's now officially a member of Lucille's family."

"Lucille will make a great mother or grandmother, whichever she chooses to call herself. Lots of food and plenty of protection. She's a real mother bear when it comes to that kid."

Belle and I sunned and watched people on the bike/walking/jogging spandex highway until Mona yelled, "I got rides here. Let's scramble those taxis." The local Air force base had been practicing the protection of our geo-political borders recently with some fast-scrambled-low-level maneuvers. *Scramble* had worked its way into Mona's taxi vocabulary.

Making a living intruded on our tanning. Well, *my* tanning. I wasn't sure how much darker the sun would make Belle's smooth cocoa skin.

I spent the afternoon moving high-school kids. Most of them were older than the boy who held up the convenience store in the morning and landed in jail by afternoon. I wondered if the inept robber went to school. One of the older kids I picked up had an interesting shoulder tattoo that I noticed when he slid into the backseat.

"So, what's the tat mean?" I asked. I like some of the more subtle tattoos, but I could never overcome the pain factor enough to actually get a rose tattooed on my butt. This one was some sort of crown. Maybe it's good to be the king.

"Why?"

"I like tats. Just curious if it has anything special to say."

"No." He leaned forward, put his finger against the back of my neck and whispered in my ear. "And bitches like you shouldn't put their faces where they don't belong."

About the Author:

When Harriet Rogers was fourteen, she picked tobacco and didn't learn to smoke for three years. When she was seventeen, she picked oranges in Israel and had Ben-Gurion's revenge for a month. When she was nineteen, she worked the night shift at the Oxford pickle factory and couldn't have relish on her hot dogs for five years. She spent ten years getting through three years of college and, while she still doesn't have any letters after her name, she can say "shit" in five languages.

She has some 2nd and 3rd place ribbons from horseback riding...and a bad back, knee and elbow from the same.

When she was driving a taxi, she started a ten-book series about a taxi driver. *Sky High Taxi* is the second book in this series.

Her mission is to make people laugh. Laughter is the soul of the human machine.

Made in the USA
Monee, IL
02 February 2020

21159244R20138